Meant
to be
More

Meant to Be Series
Book Four

By **AMELIA FOSTER**

Meant To Be More

Limitless Publishing, LLC
Kailua, HI 96734
www.limitlesspublishing.com

Formatting: Book Pages By Design

ISBN-13: 978-1-64034-885-1

Dedication

To my furbabies that offer endless snuggles and try to help me write by plopping their fuzzy feline rear ends on my laptop.

Chapter One

Dean

Present Day

The nearly decade old pop song blared from the phone in Dean's back pocket. He tossed the pitchfork to the side, slid the device out, and grinned at the glass. He knew exactly who it was before even looking because only one person had that assigned text alert. His fingers flew across the screen typing out a hasty reply.

Dean: Yep, be there in thirty.

He grabbed the leather jacket hanging on the hook inside the small office Wyatt had built into the barn and was halfway to the motorcycle glinting in the sun when he was hit with the annoying concept of reality. "Well, shit."

Once more he pulled out his phone, this time swiping until he cued up his brother's number. He tapped his foot against the red clay dirt, still slightly

1

damp from the frequent late spring showers.

"What?" The single word greeting would have been rude coming from anyone other than Wyatt Carlisle. His brother managed to embody every stereotypical expectation for cowboys including using as few words as possible for anyone who wasn't his wife, Georgia.

Despite the fact that they were related and gave each other endless amounts of grief, when it came to the ranch and everything attached to it, Dean was conscientious of giving Wyatt respect. "Jillian just landed at the airport and asked me to pick her up, do you mind if I borrow the truck?"

"As long as you and your girlfriend don't make out in the front seat. That's what the bed of the truck is for." Even with the weak cell phone reception, Wyatt's mocking tone came across the line loud and clear and made Dean roll his eyes toward the picture perfect blue sky.

Dean huffed as he marched back into the barn to collect the keys from the office. "She's not my girlfriend." *Yet*, he added in his mind where only he could hear. "And she probably has a mountain of luggage, no way it'll fit on my bike."

A not unusual flurry of excitement washed over Dean as he climbed into the front seat of the massive pick-up and slammed the driver's door emblazoned with the RA Ranch logo. Each time Jillian had come back from one of her trips into the field, serenity and joy had warred within him for top billing.

No matter her assurances and no matter how many times she returned home safely, when she left for another war-torn country, he was on edge. A scenario that had played on repeat multiple times and yet with

2

each one it had never dawned on him that there was a chance in hell he felt anything other than friendship. Looking back on it, he could admit that he was delusional. Waiting up until he got the three a.m. text or phone call confirming that she'd safely landed in Ethiopia or Colombia or the Philippines was slightly above and beyond a normal friendship. Something even her mother would never dream of doing.

"I'm such a dumbass." He chastised himself as he pressed harder on the gas pedal, flicking the signal to merge onto the highway leading to the airport. It had taken saying goodbye the most recent time to click on the lightbulb over his head that he'd fallen for her.

Dean forced himself to ease off the accelerator slightly. She would be exhausted and it would be far from the ideal time to proclaim to his best friend that he'd recently managed to pull his head far enough out of his ass to realize he was in love with her.

That thought triggered an avalanche of additional ones. Girls liked flowers and chocolate and all the romantic shit he was hopelessly incapable of delivering. And it had never been like that between him and Jillian so the very notion of planning some candlelit interlude hadn't blipped on his radar. He should figure out something special.

For a half a second he closed his eyes and groaned before he focused on the road once more and tightened his grip on the steering wheel. Despite humoring Jillian by watching reality dating shows with her, he didn't have a clue where to start with romance in the real world.

This would require asking his brothers for help and admitting that their teasing had been right. Possibly a fate worse than death.

He rubbed a hand down his chronically stubbled jaw and sighed. Later. All of that would be figured out later. Right now what mattered was getting Jillian to the soft bed she was certain to be in need of and selfishly let his eyes feast on visible proof she was home and in one piece.

He cursed the full parking lot that resulted in him circling around before finally claiming a space somewhere seemingly fifty miles from the building. Moderating his pace was an impossibility and he jogged down the asphalt and through the sliding doors, hanging a left to head to the baggage claim area.

Much easier said than done. He silently swore as he wove through the lines of people waiting at the ticket counter. The epithets were directed just as much toward himself as the crowd making his end goal harder to reach.

If Asheville housed anything larger than a regional airport he might have gone crazy trying to navigate his way to Jillian.

He scanned the crowd standing beside the carousel waiting for their baggage, an involuntary smile taking over his face when his eyes landed on red hair, haphazardly knotted on top of her head, and sun-kissed cheeks dotted with freckles.

She was safe.

She was home.

He closed the space between them in long strides, stopping only when he stood behind her. Despite her countless hours of travel, the soft scent of her soap wafted over him, tightening the band that had formed around his chest over the months she was gone when he'd finally come to acknowledge that what he felt for Jillian went far deeper than friendship.

This was Jillian. The girl he'd known since he was seven years old. The one who was damn near a fixture in every part of his life since then. Why the hell was his hand shaking as he lifted it to tap her shoulder?

"You requested a car, madam?" He affected something as close to a posh British accent as his light southern drawl would allow.

She spun to face him and in the space of half a second a dozen emotions played out across her face. Everything from delight to relief to…sadness?

What in the actual hell was that?

His next words were cut off when she launched her small five-foot one-inch frame at his much larger one. Her arms and legs wrapped around him with a vise-like grip and hot, wet drops landed against his neck. Without a moment's hesitation he held her tightly to him.

"If you say one word about me crying I swear I'll punch you, and you know I'm stronger than you."

Her hiccupped threat was ice water to his mounting concern and didn't fail in making him laugh. "Duly noted, Jillybean, but I'd appreciate knowing why you're definitely not crying right now."

She pulled back and her dark-rimmed emerald eyes reflected back the exhaustion induced by days' worth of travel across numerous time zones. "Because everything has gone to hell in a handbasket, Sparky, and you need to marry me."

***

5

MEANT TO BE MORE

Jillian

Present Day

If she hadn't been delirious from a lack of sleep she probably would have handled the entire situation far better. She would have waited to drop the news—hell, she would have made it more of a request than a demand—at least until they were in his car. Her stomach growled. Preferably after she'd had food and at least six consecutive hours of sleep...a luxury she wasn't sure she could even remember.

Playing it off as a joke wasn't an option. It was more deceitful than the actual plan she'd hatched during her nearly thirty-six hours of travel home from the small village in Sierra Leone back to Asheville.

One she'd have to talk Dean into if she had any hope of fixing everything that had shattered in her absence. But that at least had to wait until they were somewhere slightly more private than the baggage claim at Asheville Regional Airport.

Dean blinked three times, each more painfully slow than the one before. "What did you say?"

Heat licked across her face as she disentangled herself from him. "I'll..." *What? Bury my head in the sand because I am beyond embarrassed I actually just blurted that out?* "I'll explain in the car." The next best thing.

She yanked one enormous bag after another off the slowly rotating machine and lifted her brows to look at him. "Think you can fit all of this in your chick magnet?"

Ever since the first time Dean had skidded to a stop

6

in front of her house in the crimson sports car, she'd given him endless grief about choosing a car based solely on what appealed most to the female population.

The twitching at the corners of his mouth was both encouraging and concerning. She was hopeful she'd at least pushed the M word off the table long enough to collect her scattered, not fully logical thoughts before diving back in. But the mischief lighting his sapphire eyes was anything but settling.

"What do you have up your sleeve, Dean Carlisle?" She pulled up the handles of her two largest cases and wheeled them over to him, silently requesting he take them out as she repeated the action with her smaller bags and drug them behind her.

He arched a brow and cut a sideways glance at her as they exited through the sliding doors. "You propose marriage to me in the middle of a crowded airport without any notice and you wonder what I'm plotting?" He winked. "Not that I minded. I'm only shocked it took you eighteen years to see that you wanted this entire package."

Jillian rolled her eyes and muttered curses in a stage whisper that made him laugh. "Yeah, that's it. All the Carlisle men are just completely irresistible and I couldn't hold out any longer." The legs that had been cramped up for far too many hours on various planes screamed at the movement as she struggled to keep up with Dean's pace through the parking lot. "Where the hell did you park, Sparky? Timbuktu?"

"Nope." He popped the P on the end of the word as he swung her cases to a stop at the bumper of an enormous black truck that sparkled in the sun. "Timbuktu adjacent."

7

She frowned as he effortlessly lifted the bags she knew were exceptionally heavy into the bed. "This is what you drive now? Have I really been gone that long I missed the Dean Carlisle transition into adulthood? I may never forgive myself, little butterfly."

Before her brain had a chance to catch up to her mouth, Dean crowded her against the rear panel of the truck, bracing his hands on the metal ledge on either side of her head. "You demand my hand in marriage in a decidedly unromantic way and have the nerve to give me shit?" The grin on his face belied his words. Heat from the vehicle warmed her spine. "Maybe you need to watch a few more rose ceremonies to see how it's really done."

Jillian pushed his shoulder lightly and ducked beneath his arm when he didn't move. "Why don't you get in your big boy car and I'll explain what I really meant."

Dean took advantage of the extra foot he had on her and crossed in front of her to open the door before she could reach for the handle. Once she had climbed inside he slapped a palm to his chest and sighed. "Are you telling me I don't get wined and dined? Damn, you're a shitty date."

She clicked her buckle into place and dipped her chin, offering a sardonic smile. And a good natured middle finger. "Good thing you've never dated me." With that, she reached for the handle and jerked the door out of his hand, slamming it shut.

In usual Dean fashion, which was one of about a million reasons she knew she could only go to him for this kind of help, he hopped into the driver's seat and backed out of the parking space without pushing for

8

more information. Several minutes had passed as he eased back onto the highway with only silence between them. He knew her so well he gave her the time she needed to collect her thoughts. The nerves she tried to cover with the sarcastic, biting remarks so representative of their friendship ramped up with every rotation of the wheels drawing her closer to home.

Shit. Home. No, the conversation she needed to have, the massive favor she would have to beg for absolutely could not happen there.

"Do you have to get back to...whatever it is you do at Wyatt's?"

A shadow passed over his face and for just a moment his expression was indecipherable, even with nearly two decades of experience reading Dean like the back of her hand. As quickly as it appeared, it faded and a grin slipped easily into place.

"Whatcha up for?"

The childhood nickname she'd always treasured wrapped around her in a new way after her latest, and longest, absence from home. And Dean. "Fredrock?"

His impish grin grew into a broad smile as he flicked the arm of the turn signal. "I thought you'd never ask."

For the first time in more than two weeks since she'd first gotten wind of a problem, a portion of the mantle of responsibility that weighed heavily on her lifted. She settled back into the surprisingly plush seat, tilted her head back on the rest, and closed her eyes. If anyone could right her spiraling world, it would be Dean. He was the one constant she could always count on.

Chapter Two

Dean

Nineteen Years Ago

"You need to stay where I can see you, understand?"

Dean and Connor exchanged bored expressions until their father cleared his throat, then both boys stood at attention. "Yes, sir." Despite the less than two year age difference, they spoke the words in the same unified voice they did everything, behaving more as twins.

They circled the lake, discussing with as manly tones as possible the viability of fishing in the seemingly expansive crystal water. Tag morphed into hide and seek, still well within the line of sight of their father and older brothers a few yards away, walking out the best portion of land for the barn and corral to house Wyatt's horses.

Connor turned to face the trunk of a tree and buried his face in the bark. "One…two…three…"

As his voice trailed off, Dean ran to the left, then backtracked to the right. His seven-year-old face lit up when he spied a massive, flat rock he was sure he could easily hide behind. He skidded to a halt and dove behind the stone, feeling rather proud of himself.

Up until he looked to his right and directly into startled green-colored eyes. A nearly comically large bow sat atop a head of red hair exploding from her head in perfect rings. The girl's entire small body was swallowed by glittering, frothy pink fabric that shimmered the way his mother's New Year's Eve dress did when she and his father went out.

"Who are you?" The soft voice held curiosity more than recrimination.

Dean scooted a little nearer to her on the dirty ground and opened his mouth to answer, but his brother's voice steadily growing closer made him snap it closed and press his index finger to his lips. After a moment the sounds faded, but Dean intentionally kept his voice at a whisper.

The manners his mother tirelessly tried to beat into his and his three brothers' heads kicked in and he stuck out his right hand. "Dean Carlisle. What are you doing here and who are you?"

The girl's small, soft fingers curled around his, giving a gentle shake. "Jillian Leigh Monroe. I live right over there." She released her grip to point to the imposing mansion visible in the distance. "And I'm hiding too."

Dean moved his mouth closer to her ear to drop his voice even lower. "Who are you hidin' from?"

Jillian folded her thin arms over her chest with a huff. "My mother. She's having one of her fancy parties and I don't wanna be there anymore. It's boring and the people are annoying." She scrunched her freckle

11

covered nose. "And the men smoke stinky cigars in Daddy's study."

"I like parties. My last birthday Mama got a piñata," he puffed up his chest as much as he could, "and I broke it open on my second try."

She twisted her lips to the side and dropped her gaze to her lap, curling one of the many layers of her skirts around her fingers. "I've never had a piñata." Her head fell forward more. "Or a real birthday party."

Dean bumped into the rock behind him as he took a step back in shock. "Never?" He frowned at her. "Never, *ever*? With a big house like that you could have *insane* birthday parties with a hundred people if you wanted. Shoot, maybe a thousand."

Jillian peeped up at him, the green eyes he thought were so pretty when he first saw her now holding a tinge of sadness. "Mother and Daddy take me out to a proper restaurant for my birthday every year. Daddy gets lamb and Mother gets veal."

"What do you get?" He angled his leg and turned to face her, the looming threat of his brother discovering what he thought was the best hiding spot he'd ever found. "It's your birthday, you oughtta get something special like triple chocolate cake."

She shrugged slightly. "For dinner I get spaghetti, but with alfredo sauce because Mother worries that red sauce will be too messy." She turned her head slightly and the early evening summer sun glinted off the sparkling stones in her ears. "And for a present I usually get jewelry like these diamond earrings."

Girls were weird. Dean had known that ever since kindergarten when Shelly Davis chased him around the playground screaming that she wanted him to kiss her.

Just plain weird. But even still he couldn't imagine anyone, boy or girl, to be happy with a boring birthday like that. "Well, do ya at least get some cool toys?"

"I have special dolls that I keep in my room, but I have to be very careful with them. They are porcelain and very expensive."

Even though he could see the place Jillian called home in the distance, he was certain she lived in a whole other world. Maybe his parents had built their new family home on some alien landing pad. He'd have to tell Connor. That would be the best part of moving.

A man's voice called out in the distance and Jillian hopped to her feet and hastily brushed off her skirt. "That's our butler, I better go." She dipped slightly in a way that Dean had only seen on the princess movies his mother was obsessed with. "It was very nice to meet you, Dean Carlisle."

Just more proof that all girls are weird. Even his mom.

He got to his feet, then closed his eyes and groaned when footsteps thudded in the distance and Connor began crowing his delight at "finding" his brother...which was clearly not true. "Nice meetin' you too."

She tilted her head to the side. "You're pretty nice, even for being 'new money.'"

With that she took off and Dean was left scratching his head. Definitely an alien landing pad. The girl spoke in some crazy language he'd never heard before. As she took off toward the man lumbering across the yard, Dean turned and walked back to where his father and older brothers stood.

"Daddy, what's new money?"

MEANT TO BE MORE

***

Jillian

Nineteen Years Ago

Jillian slid her hand into the older man's, his firm grip both comforting and slightly annoying. "It took a lot longer for her to notice this time." She couldn't help but skip as they traveled back to her house. Certainly not from happiness at returning to the exhausting and boring luncheon her mother was hosting, but from the boy she just met.

He was nice and had a funny smile.

The gray-haired man at her side turned his head toward her, his lips twitching. "You know you shouldn't run away from your mother's party."

"Henry, what time is it?"

He turned his opposite wrist and glanced at the silver banded watch. "It's nearly five."

Jillian nodded and slowed her skip to a walk as they crossed from the thick grass to the concrete walk through the expansive, perfectly manicured garden. "Henry, I left almost two hours ago. She didn't notice I was gone for two hours."

The threatening smile disappeared from his face and his lips turned down. "Your mother is very busy, Jillian."

Even at her young age, she knew it wasn't the complete truth. There wasn't a question that her mother held a constant list of tasks that needed to be done and events like today meant that socializing was on that to-do list as a high priority. But even on the rare time that

14

Helena Monroe didn't have an auxiliary meeting, or a fundraiser for the children's hospital, Jillian knew that she didn't register on her radar.

That is, not until she needed to show her off in a frilly, fancy gown with expertly styled hair that made her look more like the nearly untouchable dolls lining her bedroom curio than a seven-year-old girl.

Jillian tugged at the older man's hand as they closed in on the door and Henry turned, dropping to a knee in front of her on his pristinely ironed black dress pants, a formal uniform her mother insisted upon for the events Helena threw under the guise of raising money for a very worthy cause, but one where the true emphasis was on networking and social climbing.

"What do you need, Miss Jillian?"

A familiar list unrolled in her mind, now slightly altered to include playing with Dean every day at the very top. Instead of voicing any of those items, she curled the list back up and tucked it into the recesses of her brain. She released his hand and turned to one side and then the other. "Did I get all the dust off my dress, Henry?"

He stood and smiled, offering a curt nod. "Yes, Miss Jillian. You look like a princess as always." He offered the crook of his arm and Jillian dutifully slipped her small hand inside as he led her through the doors.

Helena Monroe stood a few feet away, laughing the laugh that Jillian had caught her mother practicing in an effort to make it sound real. Her flawlessly styled auburn hair, nearly an identical shade as Jillian's, cascaded down in waterfall curls against her bare skin in the backless emerald gown.

At least that's what the stylist had said when he

declared Helena ready for the party. Jillian wasn't sure she understood it all. How can hair look like water?

A small wave of relief washed over Jillian just before another arrow of hurt pricked her little heart. Her absence had been briefly noticed by her mother, but certainly hadn't caused any concern. And her father was most likely holed up in his office with a handful of other men smoking stinky cigars and playing some game with cards he'd once declared was not a game for children when she'd asked to join.

Henry had been dispatched to handle it. Problem solved.

Unshed tears burned at the corners of her eyes and Jillian quickly blinked them away, an art form she'd mastered before she even begun Kindergarten. She lifted one shoulder and offered Henry a small smile before crossing the room to take up her expected residence on the hard, uncomfortable settee.

She kept her mind busy with fantastical stories of everything from heroes on horses to fearsome dragons, tamed by unlikely princesses. The time ticked by much faster as she weaved the stories in her head, lost in a wonderland while the party wound down around her.

Her mother appeared in front of her with one hand out. "Come, Jillian, it's time to say goodbye to our guests."

Jillian hopped to her feet and obediently took the older woman's hand. They stood at the door with her father flanking her other side. One by one the people who had attended the charity event, the same ones who were at every staid, boring party her mother threw, departed with light hugs and air kisses and occasional pats on Jillian's head.

When the door closed on the final departure, Helena laid a hand on her hip and turned to Jillian. "Where did you disappear to this time?"

She hesitated a brief moment before responding. "I met the new neighbors, Mother. Well, one of them. There were a lot of boys."

Her mother rolled her eyes and tossed the few locks of hair that had fallen over her shoulder. "That was…congenial of you, darling."

Jillian blinked several times, wondering what congeni-whatever was, but bit her tongue rather than ask. "Thank you, Mother." With that she pulled on her father's arm and lifted to her tippy-toes to peck him on the cheek. "I'm going to go get ready for bed now."

She raced up the stairs once she was out of her parents' line of sight. She tapped on the door right next to her bedroom. When her nanny opened, Jillian bounced on the balls of her feet. "Frieda, can I please have a bath with extra bubbles?"

The older woman smiled, cracking the lines etching her weathered face. "Of course, little princess. Run and get your pajamas and I'll have so many bubbles waiting for you that you'll need to swim through them."

Jillian lost herself in the long minutes she spent playing in the garden tub, blowing bubbles into the air, and splashing the rapidly cooling water. Finally the chill caused her to shiver and she grabbed the fluffy white towel Frieda had left behind, stepping over the ceramic side and rubbing herself mostly dry before pulling on her underwear and thin pajamas.

As always Frieda was waiting in the chair beside Jillian's bed with their latest book sitting in her lap. Jillian buried herself under the covers, holding the

17

fluffy bunny Henry and Frieda had gifted her with at her last birthday—the only real toy she'd ever received. Her eyes drifted closed as Frieda described the misadventures of a very naughty rabbit and his siblings.

Chapter Three

Dean

Present Day

The soft snore from the seat beside him pulled Dean's focus from the road to the woman slumbering next to him. A grin spread across his face, accompanied by a firm squeeze of his heart. How was it possible that he'd never been able to see that the girl who had been the one constant in his life was this beautiful?

And had somehow managed to make him fall in love when he absolutely wasn't paying attention. A small detail he'd only just realized and plotted to confess. A million scenarios had played out in his mind, but he wanted it to be perfect, and perfect took a little time.

He turned down the well-worn path leading to the lake that sat on the border between his family's property and hers. The place they met nearly twenty years ago. The place that was the spot of more than one soul-connecting conversation. Their sanctuary. Their secret place.

The corner of his mouth kicked up one notch higher as the large, flat rock that sat at the edge of the water came into view. Seven-year-old Jillian had dubbed it Fredrock and he'd never thought to question her once on why. Not then and sure as hell not now.

His fingertips itched to reach out and brush the lock of auburn hair back from her face. Once again, as it had so often over the past several weeks following the revelation that he was in love with his best friend, his stomach clenched as the one remaining logical brain cell reminded him of the risk he would be taking.

Aside from Connor, and maybe even a little more than his closest brother, Jillian was Dean's confidante. His secret keeper. The one person who managed to still believe in him when he was trying to find his place in the world. And…in his family.

Dean threw the truck into park and propped an elbow on the doorframe, stroking the two days' worth of growth along his jawline. Tanner was born with one foot in the boardroom and practically thrived with the weight of the world on his shoulders. Wyatt knew what he wanted to do with his life since he was in kindergarten and he'd worked and sacrificed to make it a reality, all without taking off the damn hat Dean planned to steal and burn one day. And Connor, next to the youngest of the four, but the voice of reason and the peacemaker since childhood, had taken his natural artistic flair and turned it into a brilliant career designing homes and offices.

Hell, even Jillian had known since grade school that she wanted to live a life that positively impacted others. She'd had a passion and a determination that Dean once thought he'd never needed and certainly would never find for himself.

It had taken far longer, and included far more failures, for Dean to finally recognize his purpose. The only regret he still held was that Jillian hadn't been there when the final piece of the puzzle slid into place. She'd been his biggest cheerleader while delivering painful levels of honesty that still echoed in his mind. And the example she'd set for him had been a massive driving force to the career he'd forged with his cousin Mat and a healthy amount of trust from Wyatt.

A major part in his confession of love would be detailing exactly how she'd impacted the path his life eventually took. So as much as it killed him, he hid the details of his work and just let her believe he helped Wyatt on the ranch.

Yeah, this was going to take a long time to plan.

He couldn't wait to take her to Wyatt's ranch and show her what her influence and encouragement had created.

He turned his head and squinted over at her still sleeping form. All of that would happen right after he got a little clarification on that whole marriage thing.

His hand hung in midair just before landing on her shoulder to gently shake her awake. Never before had touching Jillian caused a second thought, but the feel of her in his arms at the airport, an act now laced with unspoken affection far deeper than they'd ever had, had Dean steeling himself against the tidal wave of emotion he now knew she could create.

Jillian stirred slightly, rotating her head, and blinking slowly several times before finally fully opening green eyes that added an extra beat to his heart rate. "Mmm, did I fall asleep?"

Her husky tone widened the smile on his face. Dean chuckled and shook his head. "Naw, Jillybean, you were just silently solving the climate issues and it required a lot of concentration."

"How have I possibly managed to crisscross the globe without your uncanny insight guiding me, Sparky?" Her responding sleepy grin teased his rapidly fraying nerves.

If he could find a glimmer of light in the darkness and sometimes outright stupid actions of his brothers that resulted in Dean being roped into helping with their sometimes outlandish schemes to win back the relationships once in jeopardy, it was that he'd learned a thing or two. But having Jillian back in the flesh, doing all the things she'd always done, things he now saw through a very different filter, was testing his every resolve to at least attempt romance.

He might not be able to offer a candlelight evening at the base of a waterfall or rent out an art gallery and create a beautiful painting, but he sure as hell could wait until Jillian somewhat recovered from more than twenty-six hours of traveling before making such a lofty declaration. Or at the very least had a shower.

And possibly clarify what the hell the completely unemotional, unexpected airport proposal was all about.

He hopped out of the cab and rounded the front of the truck, pulling the passenger door open and offering Jillian a handout. She tightened her grip and practically drug him with her to the large rock that played a leading role throughout their friendship.

She didn't release her grip until they sat side by side, Jillian on the left and Dean on the right, exactly as they had a million times before. A dazzling smile spread across her face and Dean wondered how he'd never found it irresistibly beautiful before.

And once again he mentally kicked his own ass for being so damn blind.

"No matter where I go, I think this will always be my favorite place in the world." She breathed out the words with a reverence he completely understood.

Before his mouth ran in a direction he couldn't control, he lifted his foot onto the rock in front of where he sat and rested an elbow on his knee. "I get that I'm a Grade A specimen, but I gotta know where's this whole marriage thing coming from?"

She tilted her head back and a waterfall of auburn locks flowed over her shoulder and she groaned. "This is going to be a long story."

He shot her a wink and grinned broadly. "Lucky for you, you've got me all day."

***

Jillian

Present Day

Keeping secrets from Dean was a foreign concept, but the shame of the truth was nearly suffocating and something she wasn't certain she could share...even with him. Her gut created a new knot to add to the collection that had formed over the past two weeks.

"The simple answer is money." A portion of the truth tumbled from her lips and she barely restrained the desire to physically put a hand to her mouth and halt the flow of more words. Like the entire, ugly reality.

Disbelief settled across his face a moment before he erupted into a deep baritone laugh. "Come on, Jillybean, be serious."

She slid off the large stone and held up a hand toward him. "Just wait right there."

The short jog from where Dean still sat to the truck wasn't nearly long enough to silence the voices in her head screaming and pleading for her to trust the bond they had and disclose the truth.

Jillian closed her eyes and took a deep breath before digging through her carry-on bag for the large manila envelope she'd worn down over the past few weeks pulling the papers out and then returning them to the safety of the envelope over and over. She'd meticulously read every line, every word of the document, certain she'd find some loophole buried deep inside. Hours of reading and rereading resulted in the same conclusion: this was her last option.

She clutched the envelope to her chest and returned to him at a much slower pace. She twisted her mouth to the side as she resumed her seat beside Dean. Without the explanation, in nearly every gory, embarrassing detail that he deserved, she dropped the papers in his lap.

He looked over at her, cocking his head to one side, brows deeply knitted together. Dean opened his mouth, but before the first word could come out, she held up a hand.

"Just read it. Please."

Jillian knew the exact moment he landed on the dollar amount by the widening of his eyes...followed shortly by a coughing fit when he read the clause.

24

His gaze bounced from the paper clutched taut between his hands and her before returning back to the page. "This is a joke, right? An archaic and sadistic joke, but definitely a joke."

There were a lot of words to describe her grandfather. Most of them were glowing and loving. He might not have been the playful grandfather some of her friends at school had in their lives, but he was the one member of her family she knew without a doubt loved and supported her. Her socialite mother threw an apocalyptic fit when Jillian announced her intention to have a meaningful life where she truly made a difference in the world. Not one where charity was synonymous with pretentious galas where the bill for the event was almost bigger than the total sum raised.

However, her grandfather not only offered the emotional support for her choice, but routinely made large contributions to ensure every trip was possible. His passing five years ago heralded the greatest loss of her life. And one of the millions of times she'd needed Dean and he'd been right there.

"You know my grandfather. He was eccentric and old-fashioned."

Dean's stormy expression melted into something softer before confusion took up residence once again. "Then why would he do this?"

Jillian shrugged, helpless to answer the same question that had run circles around her mind since she'd discovered the clause. In a will she'd had no interest in until it meant saving...everything. "The only thing I could think of was that he had some crazy idea that he was ensuring I'd be taken care of for the rest of my life." She offered a small laugh that barely made it past the nerves gripping her throat. "Maybe he didn't believe I'd get married or settle down otherwise."

Several minutes ticked by as Jillian stared at the fingers knitted together in her lap, unable to meet the stare she could feel boring into her from a few feet away. She knew he had questions, hell, she did too, but she only had a few answers and even less she was actually able to speak.

Wordlessly, Dean settled beside her, sliding the manila envelope into her fidgeting hands. The early evening sun dipped behind the trees in the distance. The beginning of pink and purple tones heralding the sunset stretched across the once bright blue spring sky.

Silence was never awkward or uncomfortable between them, except for in this moment when she was asking for a blind acceptance of something so big she was certain he'd decline until she bared every detail.

"There's only one thing that doesn't make sense, Jillybean." His voice was so soft and centered she found it hard to believe it was attached to the rash, slightly conceited boy who'd been her best friend for nearly as long as she could remember.

Finally she forced her eyes to lift and meet his. "What's that?"

"How is it that the only girl I've ever known to not give a damn about money other than how many vaccines or antibiotics it could supply to countries in need would suddenly want to get married and stay married for eighteen months to cash in on an obscene inheritance?" He tempered the question with a wink and cocky grin. "Although, like I said, I get why you asked me."

Because that many zeros are what's needed to save

my family from themselves. She owed him the full explanation but she couldn't bring herself to speak the words she hadn't fully processed herself.

She turned slightly to face him, angling her knee on the smooth stone beneath them. Without a second thought she clasped his hand in hers and pulled it into her lap. "I'm asking you because you're the only man in the world I trust. And...I need the money. I know I'm asking a hell of a lot to ask you to do something this drastic and just...have a little faith in me. Trust me that I have a really good reason. I need your help."

He squeezed her hand and took a deep breath. A moment of panic surged inside her and she was certain he was about to turn her down.

"Please, Dean. I'm not asking for you to give up your life and I'm not asking you to love me." She paused as heat crept up her neck. "I-I mean not love me as anything other than your friend. I'm sure you've got a girlfriend and you don't have to give that up. This is going to be in name only. Just a legality as a means to an end."

The thumb that had been stroking the back of her hand gently stilled and he blinked slowly three times. The heavy weight that settled between them and the dark clouds that formed in his eyes both disappeared several excruciating moments later.

His playful grin, the one she couldn't resist, the one that found her breaking more rules than she cared to count over the past nineteen years, spread across his face. "Well, we've watched enough of those damn reality shows you love so much. If you aren't gonna give me a rose, the least you could do is put a little romance into the proposal."

She couldn't help but giggle, partially from exhaustion, partially from an overload of stress that she was certain would break her, and partially from overwhelming relief that she was now certain of his answer. Trusting Dean to blindly agree to help her fix her problems was a no brainer. How could she have ever doubted that he'd be there when she needed him?

Jillian hopped from the rock and took a few steps away before turning around to face him, walking backwards. "If you require romance, Mr. Carlisle, I've got you covered."

She crossed to the patch of grass that included yellow and purple wildflowers. She gathered a handful before returning to him and dropping to one knee on the soft ground in front of the stone.

"Dean Emerson Carlisle, would you do me the great honor of marrying me and being my completely legally, but emotionally fake husband for the next year and a half before divorcing me and eschewing this insane union?"

He grabbed the bedraggled flowers and clutched them to his chest with excessive dramatics that tested her ability to keep a straight face. "Who could say no to that?"

Chapter Four

Dean

Nineteen Years Earlier

The hot summer wind stung his cheeks, but Dean kept pedaling faster, reveling in the bite rather than avoiding it, the thrill of the increasing speed as he descended the hill toward the lake propelling him on. He kicked his feet backward and turned the handle, skidding to a stop inches away from the enormous rock where the pretty little redhead sat perched again.

"Hey." He lifted his chin at her the way he'd seen Wyatt do to girls a hundred times before and unbuckled the strap beneath the helmet.

She crossed her bare legs at the ankle and folded her hands in lap. "Hello, Dean."

He dropped onto the smooth surface beside her and scratched at the hair his mother had been pestering him to stop fighting her about cutting. "Why do ya talk so funny?"

Jillian tilted her head and scrunched her freckled

nose. "What do you mean? I speak very well, all my teachers think so."

Dean hopped off the bike and let it fall to the ground, not bothering to prop it up with the kickstand. "You talk like some fancy schmancy adult. Who does that?"

She dropped her gaze to her lap and ran a hand over her one piece floral print romper, ironing out an invisible wrinkle from the pristine garment. "E-e-elo—" She knitted her brows together and thinned her lips into a straight line, determination etching into her creamy skin. "Elocution is very important at my school. And definitely to Mother."

"Yeah, that's another thing." He raised his foot up until his leg was angled and draped an arm across the knee. "Where do ya go to school? I've never seen ya on the bus or in my class or even at recess."

Jillian peered at him from beneath her long lashes. "I go to Ravenhurst Academy. It's where all my parents' friends' send their kids."

He'd heard the name before and was happier than a bumblebee buzzing around a freshly bloomed flower that he didn't go there when he saw the uniforms they were required to wear. They looked hot and boring and made everyone seem like a cookie cutter of the student beside them. "You mean your friends?"

She shrugged and looked to her left, in the opposite direction of where he sat. "No, I don't have friends. Not really."

Somehow before she even spoke he knew what the response would be and a fresh wave of something he couldn't quite understand washed over him. He thought he had a rough time with three slightly overprotective and seriously annoying older brothers but he couldn't imagine the life she led. How was it possible that a girl who lived in the enormous, imposing house he could see off in the distance didn't have toys or friends?

"D'ya like ridin' bikes?" No matter what she certainly had to have a bicycle and he was sure it was a beaut that outshone even the one that Tanner had.

"I've never ridden one, but it looks fun." She leaned a little to look around him. "Although you were going really fast...is that safe?"

He slapped the heel of his hand to his forehead. Without a word he grabbed her hand and drug her off the rock and over to where his bike lay on its side. "All right, Jillybean, I'm gonna fix that. Right now."

She planted her feet and tugged on the hand he was holding, halting him from moving forward. "What did you just call me?"

Dean rolled his eyes and heaved a heavy sigh. "I like you. You talk funny and you're kinda weird since you don't have toys or friends, but I like you." He tilted his head slightly to the side. "But 'Jillian' sounds like the name of someone my mom would have over for tea. Plus you've got a freckle on the top of your nose that's shaped like a jellybean."

She clamped a hand over her nose. "I do not!" Her shrill exclamation must not have earned the reaction she hoped for when he doubled over laughing because she balled her hands into fists and propped them on her hips then stomped her foot in response. "I do not have jellybean shaped freckles!"

He crossed the few remaining feet to his discarded bike and pulled it upright. "Nope, you sure don't. Just one." He wheeled back to her and tapped the tip of her nose with his index finger. "And it's right there. But

31

I've got really good news for ya."

Jillian rolled her eyes to the bright summer sky and sighed. "Please do tell."

"That's what I'm talkin' bout. Who talks like that? My brothers would have put me in a headlock until I told them." He shook his head and twisted his lips to one side.

She dropped her head, auburn waves partially covering her face. "You're making me grateful that Brad is off in boarding school."

He wrinkled his nose and squinted at her. "Who's that? And what the heck is boarding school?"

A small smile curled her lips, but it didn't light up her face the way it had when he'd first arrived today. "Bradford Evans Monroe. The third. My brother. He's a lot older than me, he's sixteen. He goes to school a long way away, has ever since he was in seventh grade. It's the same place my daddy went and his daddy went." She lolled her head from side to side. "It's kind of like college. They live there."

The horror that washed over Dean at the idea of living far from home, and most especially from his mama's chicken pot pie, long before he was eighteen was impossible to keep hidden. "That sounds mean."

Jillian shrugged. "He likes it. He's always anxious to get back when he comes home for breaks."

Silence hung between them for several minutes and Dean struggled to come up with something to say. In that moment he wished he were Tanner because his oldest brother always knew the right thing to do. Or Wyatt who could manage to make nearly anyone laugh. Or even Connor and his ability to know when silence and a hug was the best option.

"What's the good news?"

Her soft question cut through the noise in his brain and it took several seconds before he understood what she was asking.

He forced a smile in spite of all the questions in his mind. Maybe life in the massive house in the distance wasn't the fairy tale he'd imagined the first time he'd spied it. "Jellybeans are my favorite candy." He threw a leg over the seat and pointed to the front of the bike. "Now, you sit right there and hold onto the bar between the handles."

She stared questioningly at the thin strip of metal covering the front wheel. "Are you sure that's safe?"

Something Dean hadn't felt before thrummed through his veins and he spoke with more determination than he ever had before in his seven years on the planet. "I won't let anything happen to you."

***

Jillian

Nineteen Years Earlier

Fear and excitement caused Jillian's hands to shake as she gripped the bar exactly where Dean instructed. His confident assurance had given her the strength to take the makeshift seat to begin with. She had no idea why, but she trusted the boy she'd only just met. The one who came from "new money" that her mother would never approve of her befriending.

But he was already more of a friend than any of the children who went to her school or sat in uncomfortable

33

silence with her at the various luncheons and dinner parties their parents attended.

He started off at a crawl compared to the excessive speed he had arrived at. Even still the gentle breeze kissed her skin and sent shivers of excitement rippling along her skin, causing goosebumps to form.

She tightened her hold on the metal and a firm voice washed over her from behind. "I promise you'll be safe."

Never before had she believed the truth in anyone's words.

They meandered at a slightly faster rate through the soft grass between the house and the construction zone Dean told her was going to be a barn and paddock for his older brother Wyatt's horse.

"Go faster." She couldn't believe the words came from her mouth, but she meant every syllable. She knew he would be safe, but she also knew she wanted to feel the wind tangle her soft curls into knots that would positively drive Frieda insane.

He silently obliged and moved from a snail's pace to a turtle's and she sighed at him over her shoulder. "When I said faster I meant *faster*."

A mischievous grin curled his lips and his dark blue eyes twinkled. "Whatever you say, Jillybean."

The nickname had sounded weird and slightly insulting to her ears when he'd first spoken it, but in just the space of an hour it quickly turned to something very different. As the increasing wind slashed across her fair skin, she made a promise to herself that Dean Carlisle would be her best friend forever. No matter what.

Long before she was ready, Dean slowed to a far

34

gentler stop than the skidding, dust cloud creating halt he'd skidded to when he'd arrived at the rock.

"I'm hungry." His simple proclamation caught her off guard.

And was quickly accompanied by the realization that she had been gone from home far longer than she'd told Frieda and Henry she would be gone. At least her mother and father were busy with another staid business dinner where her father could show off his doting wife and proclaim the virtues of their two children. The ones they barely knew anything about.

"I need to go back. My nanny will be looking for me." A thread of worry wove its way through her, churning her long empty stomach which chose that moment to protest the lengthy hours since her lunch with a loud growl.

Dean quirked a brow and his gaze hopped from her to his house and back to her. "You wanna call and let them know you're okay? You can just stay for dinner. My mom won't care, she cooks way too much food all the time anyway."

Jillian shook her head rapidly. "No, no, that would be rude to show up at the last minute. My mother would be so mad at me."

"You sure?" He squinted at her. "She's making my favorite dinner and it's the best chicken pot pie you've ever had."

She hesitated just long enough for Dean to abandon his bike once again on the ground and pull at her hands, backing toward the house. As he tugged her closer to the giant porch, the faint scent of savory chicken lacing the air around them tempted her inside. With a sigh she stopped fighting him and let the boy lead her into the house that still smelled of fresh wood and paint.

Within seconds he pressed a cordless phone into her hand and she dutifully dialed her home number. Once she'd reassured Henry she was safe and only at the neighbor's house, a fact his astonished voice clearly found hard to believe, she disconnected.

The dinner was a whirlwind experience with excessive chatter that was in stark contrast to the painfully silent meals she was more accustomed to. The noise level rivaled many of her parents' parties, but with a fraction of the attendees.

Occasionally the playful banter between brothers must have reached a place that even the laidback Carlisle parents found unacceptable and either one or both would pin the offensive child with a serious stare that brought about immediate obedience.

The most glaring difference, the one that did funny things to her heart, was that when Mr. or Mrs. Carlisle—they'd encouraged her to call them Mike and Tracy, but she could never—asked the boys what they'd done that day, they asked her too. In fact, they asked her lots of questions. If she was looking forward to going back to school. If she liked Ravenhurst Academy and what kinds of things she did there.

His brothers took a brief lapse in the conversation to ask her why she wanted to be friends with Dean and Jillian was certain she'd never laughed that much in her entire seven years on the planet.

Only slightly more than when Dean proclaimed he was going to get a motorcycle when he was sixteen, a point which his mother immediately shot down to which he countered with eighteen and the older woman rolled her eyes.

36

That night after Dean and his father drove her home and she snuggled deep under the covers with Frieda's soft tones reading the next chapter of their book, her mind strayed from the story to the family she just met, but already loved.

Chapter Five

Dean

Present Day

"Dammit!" He kept the epithet much softer than he wanted and drew his thumb to his mouth where he'd accidentally sliced through it with the knife he'd been using to cut a pepper. His punishment for staring at Jillian's slumbering form on his couch rather than the food he'd decided to prepare for her.

Once again his gaze found her and tracked every movement of her chest as it expanded and contracted in soft, perfect rhythm.

The lead weight that had formed when she threw out the proposal so casually rolled around. This was either a terrible or an amazing opportunity. He chewed on the inside of his cheek, the same looming threat that had stopped him from declaring his feelings for her a dozen times already hung squarely in front of him.

As quietly as he possibly could, he walked down the hall to the bathroom and fished through the cabinet for a

Band-Aid. He washed his hands in the sink and dried them off before securing the bandage in place.

He caught sight of his drawn face in the mirror and sighed. Losing her as a friend was a very real possibility when this was over. And that was a fact he wanted to ignore. He shook his head and returned to the kitchen, this time keeping his focus on cutting up the vegetables to add to the pan beside him on the stove with a coat of oil warming at its base.

That absolutely couldn't happen. Which left him with only one option: he had to make his best friend fall in love with him over the next eighteen months that they would be fake married. He rolled his eyes as he threw the strips of pepper into the zucchini and onions already sautéing in the pan. *Yeah, no big deal.*

Just as Dean turned the burner down to a lower heat, Jillian stirred on the sofa and his heart clenched. He'd missed her more than he'd ever let on.

She sat up and gave a sleepy smile. "That smells delicious." She wandered into the kitchen, fingers scratching her tousled red hair. "I can't believe you cook. It's almost like you're a grown-up, Sparky."

He drained the pasta in the colander in the sink and added it to the vegetables sautéing. "Did you miss the townhouse you've been sleeping in for the past two hours?" He waved an arm to encompass the small, but comfortable one bedroom living space. "No parents or older brothers in sight."

Jillian rested her elbows on the end of the counter and leaned in. "Speaking of which...we're going to have to tell them the truth. That this is all just a means to an end."

A small voice in Dean's head agreed with the

39

concept, but had a very different end in mind than she did. "I don't know about that, Jillybean. You know my folks." He lifted one shoulder. "They're pretty understanding and try to let us lead our own lives and make our own mistakes, but this might be too much even for them."

One finger ran across her bottom lip and she let out a small sigh. "I don't like the idea of lying to them, Dean." When she used his real name and not the nickname she'd given him when they were kids, he straightened up and paid attention. Fine lines formed between her brows. "And my parents know the truth, obviously because they know Granddaddy's will. I don't want to keep this from your family. I don't want them to think we're actually in love."

The last few words pricked his heart, but he slid his mask firmly in place.

It was a risk, and a little closer to his real feelings than he should probably get, but he took a deep breath, put the lid on the pan, and turned to face her with as playful a smile as he could muster. "C'mon, Jillybean, it isn't a lie. You know you love me." He added a wink, but internally screamed for her to agree.

Her shoulders relaxed slightly and the frown marring her creamy complexion evaporated. She closed the few steps separating them and wrapped her arms around his waist, resting her head on his chest. "Of course I love you."

Without hesitation he held her firmly against his body. His heart soared at the five simple words confirming she felt the same. Words lodged in his throat.

"You're my best friend and the only person on this

planet I could possibly trust with something like this."

And just like that, the bright flame of hope fanned by excitement that she had come to the same recognition of truth he had was extinguished. Reality was a leaden weight in his gut. He couldn't possibly blame her, it had taken him years to admit his feelings for her. It was unrealistic to think that a few minutes back in his presence would be all it took.

Although that would be a damn sight easier than the current hell of romance movie-worthy unrequited love to contend with.

Questions danced on the tip of his tongue, but if nearly twenty years of friendship had taught him anything about Jillian, it was that she'd share the details of her current problem when she was ready. Still, the girl who had never wanted the lavish lifestyle she'd been born into and only saw money as a means to save the world suddenly wanting to put her career and entire life on hold for a year and a half to land a trust fund that had been sitting dormant for five years didn't add up.

He pushed the thoughts to the back of his brain for another time and instead basked in the pleasure of her in his arms. How many times had they stood exactly like this and it hadn't meant a fraction of what it did now? How in the hell could he have been so blind for so long?

Although every cell of his body cried out against the action, he dropped his arms and pushed her away slightly. He turned to grab the dishes and give his hands something to do that didn't involve pulling her back and kissing her senseless. That might be a bit premature.

He piled her plate with a heaping mound of the simple dish and held it out to her. "Eat up, Jillybean. It

41

sounds like we're going to have one hell of a day ahead of us and it's already after five."

She took the plate and held it up to her nose, closing her eyes and inhaling deeply. "Dean Carlisle, how is it possible you aren't married?"

Because I'm in love with my best friend and don't have the spine to admit it. Yet. He shook his head and grinned, nudging her toward the table. "Now that would be awfully inconvenient if I had a wife and had to marry you too." He ran his hand along his stubble covered jaw. "Pretty sure that's illegal in this state."

The fork she had laden with vegetables and pasta hung in the air halfway between her mouth and the mountain of food in front of her. "You...actually never answered me about that. Is this really okay for you? Are you dating anyone?"

My last relationship ended two years ago when you came home for three days and flew off again and I realized three hours later that my heart was somewhere over the Atlantic and I was a complete dumbass for not realizing it sooner. His very unhelpful mind filled in the answer with a truth he wasn't ready to actually speak.

Outwardly he shook his head. "Nope. I'm free and clear and all yours to lock into wedded bliss." He filled his own plate and sat down beside her. "So, which family do we share the happy news with first?"

***

Jillian

Present Day

A fresh wave of guilt washed over Jillian at the same time as Tracy Carlisle's arms encircled her. She'd been a second mother—in reality a first in terms of emotional support and maternal affection—since she met Dean. The deception shrouding their engagement was a heavy weight. Truth danced on the tip of her tongue as she squeezed the other woman tightly. But blood deep loyalty overrode every other desire and she swallowed down the words threatening to spill out, as well as the tears skating along the edge of her lower lid, ready to fall.

"I've missed you so much, sweetie." The sincerity pouring from the few words mingled with the warmth in her touch. Tracy pulled back slightly and cupped Jillian's face between her palms. "You aren't allowed to leave until you have a good meal and tell me all about your last trip. I think Dean said...Sierra Leone this time?"

Meaningless in the grand scheme of things that Tracy Carlisle managed to remember where Jillian had most recently been sent during her time with Doctors Without Borders, but another nail in the coffin of guilt suffocating Jillian for the deceptive path she and Dean were leading his family down. *Me*, she corrected herself silently, *I'm the one doing this.*

But the small acknowledgement that her mother never even bothered to give was further proof that the Carlisle family loved her like no other. And now she was going to hurt them to save the blood relatives who were little more than acquaintances most days.

"Yeah, Mom, Sierra Leone," Dean confirmed from across the room, breaking his conversation with his father long enough to nod along with the comment before Jillian could respond. "Which means she spent something like twenty-six hours flying home, so try to lay off the interrogation for at least a day or two."

Jillian tried to purse her lips past the smile tugging at the corners. "Dean Carlisle, be nice to your mother."

Tracy chuckled and patted Jillian on the arm before leading her to the sofa in the center of the room. "Honey, after what his brothers have put us through lately, Dean's mouth is the least of my concerns."

Just before she left and the few times she'd been able to video chat with Dean while she'd been gone, he'd briefly mentioned one excursion or another to help out Tanner, Wyatt, and Connor, but he'd never gone into great detail. And Jillian knew her best friend well enough to know that he'd clue her in when he was ready. Pushing him too soon would cause a fight she had no intention of engaging in.

At least not until she'd had a decent night's rest. Then nothing would give her more joy than a little verbal sparring with Dean. Keeping his head from getting too big was one of her favorite pastimes and that usually required some good natured arguments that never really got heated. Because that wasn't who they were.

Two peas on opposite ends of a pod, his mother had called them since childhood. Only one time had they ever truly fought, but they were teenagers. Ridiculous, dramatic teenagers full of excessive emotions and uncontrolled hormones.

In some ways they couldn't possibly be more different, but in other ways they couldn't be more alike. And the deep friendship, the bond that could withstand anything, was at the center of it.

And the very reason she could ask to do something as insane as being party to a fake marriage. A small part of her still couldn't believe he'd said yes.

The very man occupying her mind slid behind her on the couch. She turned to look at him quizzically, but he merely flashed the grin that always managed to talk her into doing stupid things when they were younger.

"Actually, Mom, we have to tell you something first."

Her stomach clenched with every word he spoke, then magically seemed to settle when he lightly trailed his fingers down her forearm and linked them with hers where they rested on her knee. The small voice in the back of her brain that belonged to her teenage self that briefly thought she wanted more from her best friend when they were in high school, took over her conscious thought. She found herself wishing this could be real.

Within seconds reality took control and logical thought reined the childish ideations she thought she'd banished. This was Dean and she wouldn't do anything to risk losing him. Entertaining stupid, unrealistic emotions absolutely did that.

A spark flared in Tracy's eyes and Jillian cursed both it and the hope that created it. And the immature, careless behavior that lead to this moment.

"Jillian and I are getting married."

Silence blanketed the small group of four for half of beat of Jillian's rapidly pounding heart before the explosion of hugs and tears took precedence. Mike

Carlisle clasped Dean's hand behind her and she barely registered the muttered "about damn time" that followed as she was once again pulled into an even tighter embrace from her soon to be mother-in-law. A title she desperately wanted to cherish, but knew she had no right owning.

Tears streamed down Tracy's cheeks when she pulled back and held both of Jillian's hands firmly in hers. "I knew that you two were meant to be more than just friends."

The simple string of words played on repeat more than an hour later as they made the short, but jolting drive from his parents' house to hers. Only a few hundred feet separated the two homes, but leaving the warmth and love that radiated through the Carlisle home for the distance and sterility of the Monroe estate was jarring at the best of times.

And this was certainly not the best of times.

A new thought occurred to Jillian just as Dean smoothly parked the functional truck in front of the looming mansion and she groaned, smacking her palm to her forehead.

"What's wrong?" Dean's thick brows drew together and his head tilted slightly as he pulled the key from the ignition. The nickname that never fell away as they grew up was a soft reminder of the strength of their relationship.

"I just realized that we forgot to bring my bags. You're gonna be forced to come back to the Glass Castle tomorrow." She covered her face with her hands. "I'm making a mess of your life and I haven't even been home for twenty-four hours."

He pulled her hands gently free. "Hey, you aren't

making a mess of my life. I'm all in for this with you and it sure as hell isn't the first stunt we've pulled together." The corner of his mouth kicked up into the charming grin she couldn't believe hadn't landed him a wife yet. "Besides, do you think there is any way I'm letting my fiancée spend her first night back in the States under a different roof than me?"

"I'm not your fiancée." Despite her words, she gripped his hand tightly in hers. "Not really, anyway."

Dean shook his head. "You asked, I accepted, and now the Ice Queen gets to plan a wedding that we will both hate. Can't get much more real than that."

Jillian laughed at Dean's childhood nickname for her mother, one she hadn't heard in far too long. "All right, Sparky, let's get this over with." She released his hand long enough to climb out of the vehicle and ascend the stone steps at the front of her childhood home. At the threshold he linked his fingers through hers again and just gave a wink when she looked up at him seconds before the door opened in front of them.

As expected, her mother barely covered her irritation as she led them into the formal parlor. "Jillian, I realize this was a decision that had to be made in haste, but are you truly telling me that you couldn't find a more…suitable choice?"

A familiar ember of frustration fanned into a flame of anger. Helena Monroe knew exactly why this was happening and was one of the primary reasons Jillian was home and lying to some of the people she loved most in this world. All the things she was doing that she hated, she was doing for the mother who never showed an ounce of the care that Tracy Carlisle did. For the father who made mistake upon mistake and left it for

47

everyone else to clean up. For the cold structure that never felt like a home, but that Jillian was certain her mother treasured more than either of her children.

Even though Helena knew the truth, Jillian took that moment to pull Dean close to her side. Something not unusual for them, but with just a little more intimacy than the friendly embraces that were their norm. She fitted her body close to his and ran her thumb along his side before she snaked her index finger through the belt loop of his jeans.

"Dean isn't simply a suitable choice, Mother, he's the perfect choice for me." She beamed up into his confused face. "In fact, we only came here to let you know that if you want to plan the wedding for June as you hoped, that was fine, but I plan on staying with Dean until then."

Crimson mottled Helena's creamy, surgically stretched cheekbones. "Jillian, that is absurd. This is a *temporary* marriage of convenience simply to appease your grandfather's antiquated stipulation and..." Her words died off before she revealed the secret Jillian was certain she'd rather take to her grave than allow anyone—especially Dean—in on the greatest shame the Monroes had ever experienced. "And no one will actually believe that you, the child of one of the oldest, most well-established families of Asheville, is marrying...new money."

Jillian composed her face into the most compassionate expression she could muster and tried not to laugh along with the faint repressed rumble coming from Dean's form pressed tightly to her side. "Oh, Mother, you underestimate people. They know I'm nothing like you. But do feel free to get started on the wedding."

With that final comment, and just enough suspicion left at the validity of the engagement that was most definitely a ruse, Jillian all but dragged Dean out the door. Both of them collapsed against the side of the truck, letting the deep laughter they'd barely restrained free.

Dean sucked in a lungful of air and righted himself, a few giggles still remaining in Jillian as she swiped away a tear.

"All right, Jillybean, this night definitely requires we end it with copious amounts of alcohol."

"I like the way you think, but I don't feel like going anywhere that requires being too far from a horizontal place I can crash." She ran a hand across her belly, aching from the full body chuckles she hadn't experienced in far too long.

"Well, now, darlin'..." Dean affected a deep, embellished southern drawl nearly identical to his older brother. "Ya see, Wyatt needs a place he can drink with cowboys and get as loud as he wants and Georgia runs a mighty tight ship."

Jillian smacked Dean in the abdomen. "So what you're saying is your big brother has turned your place into a cowboy frat house."

Dean lifted his shoulders and turned down his lips. "Basically."

She pulled open the door of the cab and climbed in. "All right then, partner, let's see who's better at beer pong."

Chapter Six

Dean

Fifteen Years Earlier

"What in the blue blazes is a co-tee-lee-on class?" Dean scratched his scalp and watched the little redheaded girl softly step into the shallow water at the edge of the pond.

Her light laughter carried over to him on a warm spring breeze. "Cotillion, Dean. Kuh-till-yun." She slowly enunciated the confusing word. "And every young lady in the Chesterfield and Monroe families has always attended cotillion classes for more than a hundred years."

He hopped off the rock, tugging off his shoes as he crossed the short distance to join her, leaving a trail of sneakers and socks in his wake. "Yeah, but way back then they were ridin' horses and stuff too. Is the Ice Queen planning on giving up her Bentley for a Clydesdale?"

Jillian held her skirt above the water and carefully

moved a little deeper. "Never in a million years." She sighed heavily and tipped her face toward the sun blazing above them. "And you need to be careful calling her that. If she ever overhears you she'll never allow me to see you again."

Dean snorted. "Aw, don't worry, Jillybean. The Ice Queen would never leave the glass castle to lower herself to the likes of 'new money.'"

She stopped moving and twisted her lips to the side. "You know I don't think that...right?"

He dropped his gaze and kicked at the murky water lapping his calves. "Think what?" The question was ridiculous. He knew exactly what she meant, but despite the close bond they'd forged, he sometimes wondered why she would leave her perfect, pristine home to play in the dirt with him.

Her soft fingers landed on his forearm and drew his attention back to her face. "You're my best friend. I don't care that you, o-o-or anyone really, just came into money. I don't really care if you have money or not, honestly." She tilted her head and smiled softly. "All that I care about is that you don't cheat at Scrabble and you let me practice riding on your bike."

Cheating at Scrabble wouldn't do him any good. He was convinced that Jillian knew more words than Tanner and he was about to go to college in a little over a year. He puffed out his chest and slung his thumb through the belt loops of his shorts just like he'd seen Wyatt do. "Nope. I'd never cheat. I'm an honest man."

Jillian dipped her chin and blinked once very slowly. "Dean. You're ten years old. You aren't a man."

"If you're gonna go to that...that..." he scrunched his face up as he tested the pronunciation in his head

51

"…kuh-till-yun class and learn how to become a proper lady, I can be a man."

She opened her mouth, but before a single word could come out she let out a loud yelp. Within seconds tears formed at the corners of her eyes and she grabbed onto his shoulder.

Dean wrapped an arm around her waist to keep her from sliding into the water and getting the pale green dress dirty. Something that would certainly earn a scolding from her mother and possibly hail the end of their playtimes together. "What's wrong?"

Her grip on him tightened and she leaned into him. "Help me to Fredrock. I need to sit down." She hiccupped as a single wet path made its way down her left cheek. "I think I cut my foot on…something."

Slowly they made their way to the large, flat stone that was their designated meeting spot and he helped her lower herself onto the surface. She bunched her skirt higher on her thighs, nearly to her hips, and propped her ankle on the opposite knee to examine the bottom of her foot. The barely escaping tears turned into sobs.

"It looks so bad. I can't walk on this. There's no way I can get home." Another shuddering hiccup shook her entire body. She looked up at him with helpless, fearful eyes. "If my mom knows I got hurt here, with you…she won't let me come back."

A flurry of ideas swirled in Dean's mind. He could help her back to his house and get his mom to disinfect and bandage her foot with no problem, but he knew his mother and she'd insist on telling one or both of Jillian's parents. Stupid adult code.

Tanner was out because he was just as impossibly

responsible as their folks. An involuntary grin curled his lips. Wyatt. He was the perfect choice. Not only would his brother be willing to keep a secret, he would do a great job of fixing her up because he got cuts and scrapes all the time from getting thrown from his horses.

"It's okay, Jillybean. I know just what to do." He turned away from her and barked orders over his shoulder. "Get on."

When seconds ticked by in silence and absolutely nothing happened he rotated back to face her. "What's your problem? I said 'get on.'"

She leaned back slightly. "What do you mean 'get on?'"

He slapped a palm to his forehead. Was he really going to have to teach this girl everything fun in life? "Let me guess, you have no idea what a piggyback ride is."

Jillian lifted one shoulder, but he was slightly relieved to see that her tears had dried up.

Dean bent his knees slightly. "You're gonna put your arms around my neck and your legs around my waist. I'm gonna put my arms under your legs to hold you up and you're gonna hold onto me tight." He glared at her over his shoulder. "But don't choke me."

She stared at him suspiciously for a few seconds before doing exactly as he said. She let out a small "eep" when he lifted her, but otherwise was silent as he took careful steps toward the small barn that housed Wyatt's two horses and would certainly contain his brother. Even though they were the same age, Dean had a good four inches on Jillian. Not to mention the fact he was certain she was tinier than any of the girls in his class.

Just as the building came into view he slowed his steps. Even though she was little, the weight of carrying her up the small incline was harder than he'd expected. A small detail he would never let on to her.

He set her down on one of the barrels and promised he'd bring his brother back to help. The task took slightly more effort than he thought, but he eventually managed to talk Wyatt into cleaning up Jillian's cut and not letting the cat out of the bag to any adult...Tanner being included in that group despite the fact he was only seventeen.

After he was done, Wyatt eyed them both so closely that Dean squirmed on the bench beside Jillian where Wyatt had moved her to work on her foot. "If you two are gonna to rope me into this scheme that may land my ass in trouble with Mom and Dad, you at least should let me know why."

Despite the demand, Wyatt carefully cleaned the wound as Jillian and Dean sat in silence. Dean shrugged slightly as she looked up at him with silent, pleading eyes.

She rolled her eyes at his lack of help and turned back to Wyatt. "Because my mother is the Ice Queen who lives in the glass castle and hates new money. If she knew I got hurt while I was with Dean...she'd use that as a reason to forbid me from playing with him."

A grin spread across Dean's lips as she quoted his nicknames for her mother even as a pang of hurt pricked something inside his chest. Not seeing Jillian just wasn't an option. Instead of thinking too long on that he turned the smile to his brother. "Bonus for you, Wy. I won't tell Mom and Dad you were cussin'."

***

Jillian

Fifteen Years Earlier

"That was really nice of Wyatt to help me." She drew her brows together and concentrated on walking as normally as possible despite the spike of pain that shot through her with every step.

The silence from the usually chatty Dean churned the peanut butter crackers and apple juice Wyatt had stolen from the house when his mother wasn't looking and brought out to her in the barn after his stint as nurse on call for her injury.

In the distance she saw the sleek, black town car that her mother used glide down the driveway and out of sight. A breath she hadn't realized she was holding escaped her mouth and her shoulders dropped slightly.

She was so much more fortunate than many children, but a small stone of dread settled in her tummy the closer they drew to her house.

Many of the galas, luncheons, and auctions her mother either hosted or chaired raised money for children of some sort. Impoverished ones, sick ones, at risk ones. The pictures displayed, tastefully and discreetly as her mother always insisted, were certainly reminders that she had a much more privileged life than many. Something she knew deep down, even at her tender age, that she should be grateful for.

But the time she spent with the Carlisle family took the small, pestering questions that formed when she watched TV shows or movies featuring families and turned it into a deep cavern of want. Mike and Tracy were strict parents in some ways, all the boys knew to respect their parents and always addressed them as sir and ma'am, but their devotion to their children was undeniable.

And something she was growing to wish she had in her own, otherwise lavish world.

"You think you got this?"

Dean's abrupt question brought Jillian back to the present and she realized they were standing just on the edge of her property line. The same place Dean stopped every time he walked her home. Helena Monroe's impeccable manners had been fully in place the singular time Jillian had dared bring the boy into her home, but her true feelings were painfully obvious even to children.

The scrape on her foot ached, but not nearly to the level that she portrayed when she scrunched up her face. "Could you just walk with me to the door? I'm afraid it might hurt too much to make it all the way on my own."

He glanced from the house to Jillian and back again, squinting one eye. "The Ice Queen probably wouldn't be real keen on that."

"She's gone." Jillian piped up quickly, taking hold of his forearm. "I saw Ronald pulling out with the black town car only Mother uses."

With that bit of information, Dean shrugged and plodded forward. It didn't escape Jillian's notice that he made certain he didn't walk faster than her, letting her take hold of him when she needed a little help.

Although needed was a slight exaggeration.

Dean hung back at the door, but only required a

56

small amount of urging to come inside. Jillian scoped out the empty landscape and tugged on his hand to pull him toward the staircase that led to her room.

Once she'd quietly shut the door, she inspected her outfit in the mirror before popping up onto the frilly bedding and bouncing slightly.

Dean raised a brow at her and twisted his lips to the side. "That's a rather mir...uh...miraculous recovery."

Her cheeks heated and she turned her head away. Even though she'd much rather be with Dean and his family, there was something comforting about having him as part of her world for a change and she couldn't quite figure out why. So instead she kept her mouth firmly closed and tracked him as he wandered about her room.

He scratched his scalp of unruly brown hair. "This is a real nice room, for a girl I mean, but where's your stuff?"

She turned her head and drew her brows together, staring at him in silence for a moment. "All of this is my stuff."

Dean flung his arms out wide and turned in a circle. "Where are the toys and the games and the...ya know, *stuff*?"

Jillian pressed her lips together and pulled them both in between her teeth. "Mother feels that toys are a waste of time and that it's better to read." The slight ache in her heart turned into a few rapid thumps. "But...I do have some things I've saved. In secret that she doesn't know about."

A very excited, but very dangerous, grin turned up the corners of his mouth. "You know how much I love secrets."

She crossed the room, opened the door to the large walk-in closet, and rooted around under the shoe rack for the rectangular box she kept hidden. She brought it back to the bed and crossed her legs on the mattress, patting the spot beside her before opening the lid. Pictures, articles, and pamphlets practically erupted from the small space she confined them to.

Dean closely examined several sheets of paper before he looked up with a questioning gaze. "What the heck is all this?"

The irritation that flared inside her at every pointless dinner party thrown under the guise of raising money caught fire again. "I am so sick of my parents and all their friends pretending like they are so wonderful because they hold auctions and galas and stupid garden parties." She snorted a frustrated huff out of her nose. "They spend more on the event than they actually send to the people who need it."

He squinted at her and scratched the back of his neck. "That sounds about right from what you've told me about your folks, but...that still doesn't explain this." He waved a hand across the mess spread out before him.

"Because I'm going to go there. And there. And there. And maybe there too." She pointed at half a dozen pictures and passion blossomed in her gut. "I'm not going to send money and brag about it to my stuffy, snooty friends, I'm going to go there and help them and dig wells for water and give the kids vaccines and...I don't know what else, but I am going to do it."

Silence fell between them long enough that Jillian's stomach churned, expecting her best friend in the whole world to laugh at the private dream she held. She

58

squeezed her eyes closed tight and then dared to look at him again.

A much more genuine smile lit up his face. "If anyone can do it, Jillybean, it's you."

Chapter Seven

Dean

Present Day

Frazzled auburn hair and a blatantly pained expression should not have ignited the silent smoldering embers of desire in Dean's gut just from thinking of Jillian, but when it was combined with a practically see through shirt and nonexistent sleep shorts, it did. It definitely did.

She pressed the heel of her hand to her forehead and propped her elbow on the side of the refrigerator. "When the hell did you start playing a one man band in your kitchen at too damn early o'clock? The Dean I knew loved to sleep in."

The deep sense of rightness that cemented itself at the sight of Jillian in his bed last night after she passed out from one too many drinks warred with frustration inside him. "Eight a.m. isn't all that early considering the fact that it's a workday, and that wasn't a marching band, it's called making breakfast." He nodded toward the small round table a few feet away. "Go sit down."

She grumbled and groaned, but shuffled over to the wooden chair and slumped into it. "I don't think I could possibly eat anything."

Dean plated the omelet and grabbed the glass sitting beside the stove. He set the dish in front of her as gently as possible to avoid a loud clatter that would undoubtedly cause her already throbbing head to riot more. "You need to at least try. This is my famous hangover special, after all. It's solved more morning after regrets than I can count…and not just mine."

She sipped on the Bloody Mary and peeped up at him with one bloodshot eye as he took the seat next to her. "I thought your regrets usually came in D cups with bleached blonde hair."

The regretfully accurate barb pricked his conscious. As always he pushed aside the real emotions and relied on a dramatic chest clutch. "Why, Jillybean, you wound me."

She twisted her lips to the side for a moment before shoving a small forkful of the veggie laden omelet in her mouth. "No woman has ever hurt the untouchable Dean Carlisle."

He swallowed back the involuntary laugh that bubbled up in his throat. The woman was damn near killing him right now with this whole fake engagement bullshit and she had the nerve to say that? With more sincerity than brain cells, he shook his head. "You aren't just any woman. You're my best friend." He pulled himself together enough to toss her a cockier-than-he-felt grin. "And my soon-to-be wife."

"Temporarily. Only eighteen months." She waved her fork in his direction before spearing more food.

"Give or take."

A fleeting glimmer of hope fluttered behind his breastbone like a delicate butterfly. "Give or take?"

Jillian looked from her plate to the wall to the sliding glass door on the opposite side of the townhouse that led to the small back deck. Everywhere but directly at him. Normally a bad sign, but one that couldn't help but feed the lovesick beast inside him that he practically loathed at times.

He curled a finger under her chin and pulled gently to bring her to face him. "Don't you think your fiancé deserves a little more explanation there, Jillybean?"

Her green eyes disappeared behind her lids for several seconds before she brought her gaze to meet his. "We have to stay married for eighteen months for me to access the trust fund, but then there is a process of actually getting the money as well as the divorce proceedings so..." Her voice trailed off on a sigh. "There's a chance this fake marriage could last a couple of years."

A completely inappropriate smile begged to break free across his face and Dean coughed a few times to try and hide his glee. "Two years?" Hell, in that length of time making Jillian fall for him was damn near a given.

"Listen." She laid a hand on his forearm and turned to face him. "I don't expect you to give up...anything for me. Asking you to stop dating, stop having fun, stop...well, being Dean Carlisle for me isn't fair. You're still free to do whatever you want. This is a name only thing."

Bullshit and *hell no* raced through his mind, but he kept the words as far from his tongue as possible. He was thankfully saved from saying more by a loud alert from the phone in his pocket that had Jillian moaning and clutching her skull so tightly her knuckles whitened under the pressure.

As quickly as possible he slid the device out, swiped across the screen a few times, and clicked the button on the side to silence it. "Sorry, that was Mat letting me know he was out front."

Jillian squeezed her eyelids into slits open enough to barely show a small strip of her irises. "Mat? As in your cousin Mat? What the hell is he doing here and why the hell is he picking you up?" She groaned again and completely closed her eyes. "And since when did you make an air horn your text tone?"

Dean chuckled and rubbed her back. "He works at the ranch with me. I'm having him pick me up so you can rest. Bring the truck out when the parade in your head ends." When she finally looked at him again, he gave her a wink and grin. "Then we can bring my bike home. You'll love it."

She gently massaged her temples. "I am in far too much pain to actually ask the questions I am certain I should be asking." She took a slightly larger sip of the Bloody Mary and downed the two tablets he'd laid out beside the glass. "I'm going to attempt to finish at least half of this and go back to bed. Am I on a timeline here, Sparky?"

The childhood nickname widened the smile on his lips. "Whenever you feel better, come out. I'll text when I'm leaving if I don't see you before then okay?"

Dean waited until she'd taken another bite of the food before getting up, sliding on shoes that were much nicer than he normally wore to work, and slipping out the door. Within seconds he had hopped into the truck beside Mat. "Thanks for this, bro."

The other man carefully backed out of the narrow driveway before responding. "You realize that you have three actual brothers who are all happily married and probably a lot better at this than your divorced cousin, right?"

"Listen, Sherry was a—" Dean managed to stop talking before the word that was so accurate, but also so insulting, to the woman Mat probably still cared about came out. "You're better off. Seriously, you'll find someone else. And...I am better off without my brothers knowing anything about any of this. It's a friggin' mess until I can get her to see that it doesn't need to be."

Mat sighed and hit the right turn signal with a little more force than necessary. "So where to first?"

Dean rubbed the back of his neck and looked out the window before facing Mat again, his cheeks burning with the knowledge he'd left out a few important details. "Before you say anything, I already talked to Wyatt. He knows we're going to be late today and I know you don't have any clients booked until one..."

His cousin groaned loudly. "What are you getting me into here, Dean?"

"Mini road trip?" He held up the directions on his phone, already being called out by the slightly robotic female voice.

Mat uttered a string of curses under his breath, but took the device from Dean's hand and slid it into the phone mount attached to his vent. "I better at least get a decent lunch for this."

"I'll pick something amazing. And I'll buy." Dean

held up three fingers, his pinky and thumb touching at his palm. "Scout's honor."

His cousin merged onto the interstate smoothly before shooting him a disbelieving glare. "First, you're gonna be broke by the time this little errand is over, and second, you were never in the scouts."

Dean chuckled but didn't argue either point. Just because he worked at his brother's ranch and spearheaded a unique and highly recommended program there didn't mean he was as comfortable as his siblings. But he was smart with his money, and aside from the tricked out motorcycle, he put a decent chunk in his savings account every month.

One thing he held in common with both Wyatt and Connor was the fact that they did things on their own without the financial backing of their parents...aside from the sports car they gifted him for his graduation. Even if that meant struggling sometimes.

Being broke was a bit of an exaggeration, but his savings would take a small ding. And he really couldn't think of a better reason.

***

Jillian

Present Day

Jillian fumbled with the phone blaring out a calypso rhythm, her blurry eyes struggling to focus on the screen. When her sleepy vision righted itself, she groaned and swiped across the glass screen to connect the call. "Hello, Mother."

"Don't tell me you're still lazing about. It's nearly two in the afternoon."

Her mother's shrill voice combined with the realization that she'd slept another six hours after Dean had left was better than a bucket of ice water. She cleared her throat and jumped from the bed, thrilled her headache was gone when her feet landed firmly on the hardwood floor.

She rummaged through the small bag that housed her essentials, desperately seeking a toothbrush and toothpaste to rid her mouth of the lingering aftertaste of beer mixed with the Bloody Mary and omelet. How the hell had Dean managed to talk to her with breath this lethal?

"Sorry, Mother, I'm still operating in a vastly different time zone. Did you need anything specific?" Locating the small items felt like finding gold and she clutched them to her chest and raced to the bathroom.

The older woman cleared her throat in such an exaggerated way Jillian rolled her eyes as she applied the thick paste to the brush. "Well, I've secured the club two weeks from now for this...wedding." She paused just long enough to make her disdain apparent. "You were making some sort of ill-fitting joke by calling this entire thing real...weren't you?"

As much enjoyment as Jillian got from tormenting her mother with the idea that she and Dean were getting married for real, she didn't want the woman to have a heart attack. And despite all her faults, Helena had been through a hellacious few months. The family fortune and high social standing that meant nothing to Jillian meant the world to her mother. Even though she couldn't understand it, she also couldn't turn off the stirring of empathy.

"No, Mother, you know exactly why I'm getting married and you know the validity of it." She scrubbed her teeth for a few moments and spit out the excess foam in the sink. "But you also need to remember that Dean is bailing us out by agreeing to this. His entire life is being upended by going along with this ridiculous ploy to appease Grandfather's insane and archaic stipulations."

Helena huffed on the other end. "I still can't believe Silas Murphy agreed to write such a preposterous will."

Jillian finished freshening her mouth, swished some water, and sent it spiraling down the drain. "That doesn't really matter at this point. We are in this situation and the only way to access the funds you need is through Dean." She pressed her lips together for a moment and summoned a brief flare of will. "And I expect you to remember that and treat him kindly from now on. Especially considering the fact that your own son is barely even answering your calls and certainly hasn't stepped up to help in any way."

"First of all, it sounds like you're brushing your teeth, which is exceptionally rude to do while on the phone. You've apparently lost all sense of decorum out in that...wilderness. Secondly, Bradford sunk every dime of his half of the inheritance into his business, and with the time difference in Thailand, it's unrealistic to expect him to be in contact regularly."

Jillian rolled her eyes at her mother's familiar excuses for her brother's absence. "It's Sierra Leone, Mother. An actual country. Remember? You've done fundraisers to dig wells—"

"Yes, yes, fine, the bush." Even though they were

only on the phone, Jillian was certain her mother waved her hand dismissively with the comment. "And I've always been kind to your little friend. Even though he comes from *new* money."

Jillian rolled her eyes so hard she was afraid she'd incite the return of the headache that had plagued her all morning. "I don't mean cordial, Mother, I mean nice. Friendly even." She held a breath for a moment. "And his parents, his entire family, they...they don't know why. I thought it wise to keep those who know the truth to a minimum considering the circumstances."

It was a lie, but one she knew would be effective. Her mother would rather die than have it widely known the Monroe family teetered on the edge of financial disaster.

Some strangled sound from her mother answered before any words did. "Of course I'm not going to say anything. This isn't exactly happy news. Well, not for me. Possibly for Priscilla Gordon."

"I assume you're planning everything, yes?" If Jillian had her way, if this had been her real wedding, Helena wouldn't have come near any of the plans. But the wedding, like the marriage, was simply for show. Even still, a small corner of her heart ached at that fact.

"Darling, you may be my daughter, but your taste is...questionable. Naturally, I'll be handling all the details. I'll send you information about your dress fitting tomorrow."

With that, Jillian offered her mother a hasty goodbye and typed out a rapid fire text to Dean asking what time to pick him up. She grabbed clothes from her suitcase before hopping in the shower. Appreciation for hot water never waned and she took a few moments to let the nearly scalding spray wash over her body before scrubbing herself clean and stepping out to wrap a towel around herself.

She grabbed her phone and grinned as his face looked back at her, notifying her that he'd sent a message.

Dean: I'll be done around five thirty, but take your time. I'm attaching the directions to Wyatt's ranch. The keys are hanging on the hook by the door. Feeling better?

Her fingers flew across the screen.

Jillian: Much better thanks to your miracle cure and a few uninterrupted hours of sleep. Have great news for you, our wedding date is set. Aren't you thrilled?

A dancing cow gif popped up within seconds and nearly caused her to double over with laughter. No matter what was going on in her world, Dean always managed to make her smile. It was one of the first things that cemented their unusual friendship.

By the time she'd dressed and rummaged through his refrigerator and cupboards to find something to eat, it was nearly five and she wanted to head out early since she'd never visited Wyatt's dream-turned-reality. She pulled her long auburn waves back into the practical ponytail she sported nearly every day and grabbed the keys from the hook before exiting the townhouse and locking the door behind her. Even with the running boards offering a boost, she still had to climb into the high cab of the truck.

The GPS on her phone guided her to the ranch easily and she parked near the paddock watching Dean from a distance as he showed a man that was probably twice his age how to harness one of the horses. He gave the older guy a pat on the back and lifted his head just in time to meet her gaze and offer a smile.

The same smile that once-upon-a-time gave her butterflies. For that brief period in high school when she childishly entertained the notion that she was in love with her best friend. A crazy train of thought she was thankful she hopped off before she did something stupid and lost the single most important person in her life.

A spear lodged itself directly in her heart. The single most important person after her grandfather. His loss, though years earlier, was still so fresh to her. Even if his antiquated beliefs, combined with stupidity from her family, were the reason she was here grinning like an idiot as Dean jogged over.

"Any trouble finding it?"

Jillian shook her head, annoyed that a few strands of her unruly hair were already escaping. "Nope. Are you ready to go yet?"

A wide smile spread across Dean's face and he shook his head slowly. Jillian immediately narrowed her gaze in response. That shit-eating grin could only spell trouble with a capital T.

He eyed her up and down, giving an approving nod to the denim shorts and teal t-shirt. "Glad to see you dressed just right. I've got Honey all saddled up and ready to go." He winked. "Fredrock is an easy ride from here."

It hadn't dawned on her until that exact moment

because she'd been so focused on making all the turns the robotic voice from her phone commanded, but in her mind's eye she could picture the patch of land that now housed Wyatt's ranch and realized it was just adjacent to the home where Dean had grown up, and hers as well by default.

She easily scaled the two logs of the fence separating them and landed in front of him on the dusty ground. "Why the hell didn't you say so sooner?" She scanned the half a dozen horses enclosed with her. Only one had a saddle, and with the warm, earthy tones of the coat, it was easy to see why it would be called Honey.

Jillian looked up at him with a mischievous grin. "I'm riding in front."

Chapter Eight

Dean

Fourteen Years Earlier

"He loves me, he loves me not. He loves me, he loves me n—"

"Aren't you a little old for that?"

Jillian's head snapped up at the tone Dean had intentionally made as mature as possible, far more than his thirteen years on the planet should have allowed. "Aren't you a little immature to be so bossy?"

His steps toward their sacred rock where Jillian sat with the half destroyed purple flower still in her hands halted. He straightened his posture to his full height and pulled his brows together. "You're gonna lose that invitation to eat dinner at my house whenever you want if you keep sounding like my brothers."

She lifted one shoulder and returned to pulling the petals free one at a time, but this time remained silent. Once it was empty she tossed the stem near the edge of the pond. "You act like I'm not the baby of the family too."

Dean snorted and plopped down beside her. "You aren't. You're an only child."

Jillian rolled her eyes and twisted her head to look at him. "Let me remind you of Bradford. You know the tall, strawberry blond guy in the ginormous family portrait hanging in our formal room?"

An involuntary grin at Jillian's proper and refined tongue saying something like "ginormous" spread across his face and he gave himself a small pat on the back for opening her up to something a lot more fun than stuffy dinner parties he still couldn't figure out how she survived. "Yeah, technically you have a brother, but he's never around. He's been in that hoity-toity boarding school for as long as I've known you."

He scuffed his sneaker on the surface of the rock. "He doesn't live to pick on you and push you around like my brothers."

Jillian grabbed his chin and an uncharacteristic fierce expression colored her face. "I tell you all the time, but you need to actually listen." The corner of her eye sparkled in the spring sun. "You have an amazing family. Sure, your brothers are assholes sometimes, but all siblings are. You are sometimes too. But they love you. They'd do anything for you."

The truth of her words cemented in his gut. Yeah, the four boys brawled more than their mother wanted, but after a few rounds, whatever had been between them disappeared and they'd go back to being each other's closest friends. Especially Connor. Being so close in age and the last two of the tribe had created a special bond between the brothers similar to the one shared between Wyatt and Tanner as the two oldest.

The glittering drop that had been threatening to spill over ran down her cheek. "And I would give anything for my parents to love me the way yours do. The only one who does is Grandpa and he…"

Silence was far more concerning than whatever words she hadn't spoken. He gripped her upper arms. "What, Jillybean?"

She lifted one shoulder and sniffled. "Daddy says he'll be fine, but he's been in the hospital a long time and I keep hearing my mother mentioning his heart to friends, but she stops talking as soon as I get close enough to find out what she means."

Dean wiggled on the stone slab as he watched a few errant tears trail down her cheeks.

He wished he were Tanner. His oldest brother had a way of always knowing what to say or do. It was annoying.

He wished he were Wyatt. He might not say the right things, but Wyatt always managed to make people smile. It was frustrating because it was nearly impossible to stay mad at him.

He wished he were Connor. Though only eighteen months separated them in age, they were practically as different as night and day. The older boy had a weird way of calming anyone he was around…especially girls. It was a trait that worked in all the brothers' favor when Connor managed to smooth over whatever someone had done to irritate their mom.

Instead Dean caught one of the discarded petals from the rock. "So who loves you?"

Her dark green eyes clouded in confusion. "What in the world are you talking about?"

The question was punctuated with a much softer

74

sniffle that encouraged Dean to press on, hoping for distraction if he couldn't manage to comfort her. "I counted when you finished. You ended with 'he loves me.'"

Her freckles blended into the red coloring her cheeks as she dipped her head and turned away. "It's...it's nobody."

She hopped off the stone, brushed dirt he certainly couldn't see from her clothes, and lifted one hand. "I'll, um, see you later."

With that she raced off toward her house and quickly melted from a retreating figure to a speedy blur he could barely make out in the distance.

Dean pressed his lips together and shook his head, huffing through his nose. He dug around in the grass and dirt nearby until he found half a dozen smooth stones and expertly whipped them into the pond, smiling as the first skipped seven times across the water.

"Girls," he mumbled to the next rock he turned in his hand, "I will never understand a single one of 'em."

***

Jillian

Fourteen Years Earlier

For the tenth time that morning Jillian wished Dean went to the same school as her. The upper class, private school with the annoyingly uncomfortable uniform would be far more tolerable if he were there to crack an irreverent joke or goad her into using the kind of

75

language that would shock her mother, even if the swear words were all ones she'd heard Helena Monroe utter more than once when frazzled from a planning meeting or irate with one of the "friends" she air kissed at every function.

Jillian snorted. With friends like the ones her mother had—and the kind Helena herself was—she didn't need enemies.

She neatly filed her notebook in her locker between two thick textbooks and pulled out the ones she needed for her final two classes of the afternoon. Just as she looked up to close the door, she caught a glimpse of ash blond hair and her stomach involuntarily flipped.

Tristan Randolph.

He managed to make the khaki pants and navy blazer of the school uniform look like something out of a teen heartthrob magazine. He stood half a head above the other boys that circled around him, leeching off his popularity and status.

And he was also completely oblivious to Jillian's very existence, save for the few times they were pushed together at social functions their mothers co-chaired. Because naturally a Monroe daughter would want to be with a Randolph son. It would be a match made in social status heaven.

Tristan turned a brilliant smile on one of his friends and Jillian sighed, leaning against the metal door that latched shut at the pressure of her shoulder on it. He was the one thing she would easily acquiesce to her mother's desires if he showed her the slightest interest at all.

But she didn't have perfect blonde curls or straight chocolate brown hair. She was the shortest girl in her class…again this year. And fiery hair combined with dark, emerald eyes wasn't the standard of beauty that boys sought after.

Not to mention the freckles that dotted her cheeks and nose.

With her ever increasing crush pushed firmly back into the "never gonna happen" place it belonged, she turned on her heel and headed to one of her last classes of the day. Maybe her mother would let her visit Dean and—

A hand on her shoulder halted her footsteps and her train of thought. She spun around, fully expecting Missy or Lila to be putting on their fake friendship act to get Jillian's help with one of the classes they shared. Instead she was met with sparkling cornflower eyes and a million watt smile.

Tristan freaking Randolph stood two feet from her, not because his mother and hers had forced them together at some event that they called a fundraiser, but was truly nothing more than a social gathering.

No, there was no one standing behind Tristan shoving a lemonade in his hand and giving him talking points in hushed tones. He had sought her out all on his own. A fact that would be immediately going into her diary the second she got home.

"Hey Jillian." The lopsided grin mirrored that of the latest teen singing sensation who sent thousands of girls into screaming fits. But on Tristan it looked even better.

Her brain sluggishly remembered that she needed to speak after several moments had ticked by. "Hey, Tristan." *Stellar conversation*, she chastised silently.

He looked down for the briefest of moments and

then back up, his gaze locking on hers and a nearly irresistible smirk firmly in place on his lips. "I was wondering if I could come over to your house today and hang out for a little bit." She opened her mouth, but before she could speak, he held up a hand. "I've already cleared it with my parents."

For the first time since birth, she was grateful for the composure that her mother had drilled into her. The ability to hold a perfect smile no matter what was going on inside her brain and heart. It was the only thing keeping her from jumping up and down and making an absolute fool of herself...and probably having Tristan change his mind.

"That would be lovely." She affected her best congenial tone and laced it with a genuine smile, but not too big. Just right.

Her hand mechanically took all the notes as her teachers droned on, but her mind was far from focused on the lessons, instead planning every detail of her time with Tristan. By the time Henry arrived to pick up both Jillian and Tristan, she had mentally scheduled out the entire evening to include a romantic comedy followed by a horror flick for maximum effect.

She was certain she could fake fear well enough to incite Tristan's naturally chivalrous tendencies, the ones she was sure he possessed even though she'd never actually seen them in action, to comfort and protect her. Which would undoubtedly lead to their first kiss.

On the short drive to her home, she frowned as Tristan sat pressed against the door, seemingly as far from her as possible. He kept flicking his wrist to check the time on his watch and sighing.

Their feet had barely crossed the threshold when he

looked at her for the first time since they'd left school "Bathroom is that way, right? Last door on the left?"

Jillian's lower lip jutted out at the practically absurd question, but she nodded and watched in confusion as he darted off. Moments later he appeared again, his uniform long gone and ripped jeans, Converse, and a gray t-shirt taking its place.

He pulled his cell phone from his pocket, tapped on the screen a few times and slid it in the back pocket of his pants. "I told *Mother*," he rolled his eyes and exaggerated the word, "to send the driver over about ten so I'll be back about fifteen minutes before that to change and act like I've been here all night."

Uncertainty and shock swirled in her brain like a dense fog, stealing all the questions that stood on the tip of her tongue, begging to be asked.

Tristan leaned forward and kissed her on the cheek. "Thanks so much for being my cover, Jillian. I knew I could count on you."

With that he bolted out the front door and down the granite steps. Tears fell from her eyes at the same pace as his feet landed on the stone as he made his escape. Large, fat drops that condemned her stupidity for believing Tristan had any interest in her whatsoever.

She sniffled and wiped her nose on the sleeve of her jacket, taking the stairs to her room two at a time, shedding the stiff uniform and pulling on the closest thing to casual clothes she had. She carefully tip-toed through the house, swallowing back the emotions in case anyone saw her. As soon as she was convinced everyone was occupied, she fled out the back door and straight toward her sanctuary.

Fredrock and Dean.

Chapter Nine

Dean

Present

"Hot water, fast food, and this spot. Not in that order." Jillian wrapped her arms around herself and ended the statement with a blissful sigh.

Dean looked over at Jillian as he pulled items from the saddlebags. This was a trick Wyatt had used on Georgia, and based on her stomach swelling with their second child and the absolutely disgusting way they still acted like newlyweds more than two years later, it clearly held some merit. "That's...an interesting list."

She laughed and tipped her face to the sun, the rays kissing the freckles that had doubled in number since he last saw her. "The things I missed while I was gone, doofus."

Don't say it, don't say it, don't say it. "What, you didn't miss me?" *You are an incurable dumbass.* His mouth was going to screw everything up and send her sprinting back to Ethiopia or Honduras before he could blink.

She turned back to him and blinked a few times, the corner of her mouth curling into a half smile. "You're a given, Sparky. You know you and Fredrock are a package deal." Her eyes widened as he shook out the blanket and spread it across the stone slab. "What is that?"

"Don't tell me you've been out in the field for so long you've forgotten what a picnic is." He looked up at her and grinned as he smoothed the thick material on the smooth stone surface. He'd leave out the tidbit that it was the same one Tanner had used on Izzy and Wyatt had used on Georgia, and that he hoped it carried some weird Carlisle family magic.

And he'd made sure to wash it twice after he snagged it from Connor because he didn't even want to imagine what kinds of things this poor piece of cloth had seen.

Not that he'd ever be sentimental enough to believe in that kind of garbage like a lucky love talisman. That was Connor's thing. He was "the sensitive one."

Dean carefully pulled each container of food from the saddlebags as Jillian took a seat on the blanket and her eyes grew wide at the seemingly endless supply.

Score one for Izzy. His sister-in-law had done little more than give him a half second long knowing look before agreeing to pack up dinner for two.

The small dimple Dean had found himself thinking about in the middle of the night appeared on her left cheek. That alone was worth the endless hours of harassing "I-told-you-so's" his brothers would undoubtedly pour on him.

And, damn it, they were right.

Since Dean and Jillian first met his brothers would bump his shoulder with their larger ones and say her name in a sing-songy voice that irritated the hell out of him. They'd make kissy sounds and hum *Here Comes the Bride* when they saw her coming toward the house.

If it weren't for the fact that he loved the woman sitting next to him so much he wasn't sure he could take his next breath without confessing it, he'd hate the fact he was proving all their taunts were right. Well, right as long as Jillian agreed to make the fake engagement something a little less than fake. Something that was kinda like forever.

Her smile vanished as she popped the lid off of one of the containers and her mouth turned down at the corners. "Dean, I don't eat chicken." She lifted her eyes from the breaded planks to meet his. "Remember? Vegetarian?"

It was a fact he knew well and so did Izzy. And just in case she'd forgotten he'd reminded her. Twice.

He picked up one of the pieces and held it close to her lips. "I remembered. This is fake chicken. And I gotta admit it doesn't taste half bad."

She opened her mouth and took the proffered food, closing her eyes with a small moan that sent Dean's mind straight to the gutter. "Damn, Sparky, this is good."

His incredibly proper and refined fiancée managed to devour more food in the next ten minutes than he could even attempt. The brown leather belt was digging into his stomach and he held up his hands calling "uncle" while she plowed through two more helpings.

"Where in the hell do you put it all, Jillybean?" He wasn't sure if he was more in awe or jealous of her appetite, although the way she licked the strawberry juice from her fingers was enough to wipe both thoughts from his mind and set him on a very different track.

She lifted her shoulder and popped one more grape in her mouth before snapping the lid closed on the nearly empty container. "Working out in the sun and walking all over creation has a way of making a girl grow her appetite." She sighed and tilted her head to one side. "I'm not saying this wasn't delicious and I definitely don't want to sound rude, but tell me what this is all about."

Show time.

He grinned and pulled the bouquet of daisies, asters, and chrysanthemums all in vivid purple tones from behind the rock where he'd stashed it earlier. Her mouth fell open slightly but he held up one hand. "This is an eco-friendly bouquet from a fair trade farm. No plants were harmed in the making of these flowers."

A warm smile curled her lips and she pulled the fragrant blooms close to her nose, inhaling deeply. "Dean, they're gorgeous." She drew her brows together and frowned at him over the petals. "Seriously, what are you up to?"

He slid off the rock and knelt beside Jillian, pulling the ring from his front pocket in a move he hoped looked far smoother than he felt. He lifted the lid and did a small inner cheer at her sharp intake of breath. Without the slightest input from his foggy brain, he tucked a thick auburn wave behind her ear that had escaped her ponytail.

"Jillybean, just because this is all happening as a means to an end..." The words nearly lodged in his

83

throat. He wanted more than a fake engagement, but now wasn't even close to being the right time for that particular announcement. "Well, you're still my best friend. And you're still that girl who cried over those stupid reality show engagements even though you knew they'd be broken up within a month."

He plucked the ring from the blue velvet and slid it on her ring finger. "And my best friend deserves a real engagement ring." He slid his knuckle under her chin and lifted it so she'd look him in the eyes. "Conflict free and ethically sourced with all the proper certification to prove it."

She sat motionless, eyes glued to the ring, mouth still hanging open in shock. After countless moments that had Dean believing he had royally screwed it all up, she lifted her gaze to meet his, tears sparkling in the corners of her eyes. "Someone is going to be really lucky to get you for real one day, Sparky."

Dean smiled up at her despite the ache in his heart at the suggestion there could be anyone other than her. "For the next two years this is real. I know what you said, but I already told you I don't have a girlfriend and I'm not going to look for one." He gripped the hand he still held firmly in his.

Jillian tugged free from his hold to wrap her arms around his neck. "I can't possibly thank you enough for doing this. I'm asking so much of you and you just…jumped in to fix the disaster that's my life without asking questions." She pulled back and sniffed, wiping her forearm across her eyes. "And you haven't even pushed to know why."

He rose from his spot on the ground to the smooth stone slab, not letting her out of his arms as he moved.

"You'll tell me eventually. You always tell me everything." He placed his palm on the side of her head and gently coaxed her to lay against his shoulder. "And if you don't, I have ways of making you talk."

"This is probably exactly why none of your ex-girlfriends actually believed we were just friends. Or your brothers." She lightly pinched his side. "And you aren't that good of an interrogator."

The immediate grin that took up residence on his face at her joking challenge was completely involuntary. He walked his fingers from where they rested near her hip bone up to her ribcage and around her back before dancing lightly across the thin material barely covering her skin. "I'm pretty sure I won every tickle fight we ever had."

She squealed and leapt from the rock and spun on her heels to face him, index finger pointing at him accusingly despite the grin plastered on her face. "Gotta catch me first." She turned and raced away, Dean giving chase. She disappeared into the woods a few yards away that stood as a barrier between the house she grew up in and Dean's childhood home.

Despite his much longer legs, she managed to stay a fair distance away. He lowered his head and kicked his burning limbs into overdrive as he closed the gap between them. He barely grazed her back and gasped out, "Uncle."

Jillian turned and jogged backward a few extra feet as Dean hunched over and gripped his knees. "What's the matter, Sparky, can't handle a little game of tag anymore?"

He held up one hand and swallowed in between pants, desperately pulling air into his lungs. "I touched you, you're it." He looked up at the sky turning brilliant shades of pink, purple, and crimson as the sun began its descent. "But it's going to get dark soon and we need to get back."

She walked back toward him with a sympathetic "tsk" and patted his back as she passed. "It's okay, I won't tell your brothers a girl outran you."

***

Jillian

Present Day

For the ninth time in just the last hour, Jillian held up her left hand in the small amount of light that seeped into the bedroom from the light outside the window. Even in the dark, the emerald at the center of the rose gold band shimmered and the diamond accents twining around on either side sparkled in return. It was a breathtaking ring, but it meant more given the circumstances.

She turned onto her side on the bed, completely incapable of finding a comfortable position despite the downy soft bedding and body hugging mattress. She assumed sleep was eluding her because of the zillions of time zones she'd hopped in the past seventy-two hours, but if she were honest, that was only one component.

Dean had been her best friend for nearly two decades and she knew without a doubt when her mother first contacted her, completely panicked, that Dean would be there for her even if this was a crazy idea.

86

And he had been.

She spun the ring on her finger again, a small corner of her heart aching at the fact she'd have to give it back when their charade was up. It was perfect. Exactly what she would have wanted from a fiancé if she were really engaged.

But that was Dean. Even though he'd been dragged, albeit rather without too much struggle, into a situation he didn't ask for and didn't even fully understand, he'd managed to do something for her. To make her feel better and to make her happy.

She flipped over to her back again just as a new thought managed to penetrate the Helena Monroe induced fog that had been clouding her brain for weeks. Jillian slapped the heel of her hand to her forehead and groaned. She was being an ass. Not only was she asking a hell of a lot from Dean, she hadn't even bothered to talk to him about...him.

Their communication over the past several years had been unsatisfactory at best. She had only been stateside for brief periods of time, and texting and Skype calls didn't exactly allow for meaningful discussions.

She knew Dean was working with Wyatt, but she had no idea exactly what he did for his brother. All of the Carlisle boys were happy to be outside and Dean embodied this with his love of being dirty, digging for worms, and fishing in the pond. But he wasn't passionate about horses and rodeos like Wyatt so she couldn't imagine how he fit in on the ranch.

Especially with a degree in...

She pulled the pillow over her head and growled against the material. Some best friend she was, she couldn't even remember what his major was. In her defense, he'd changed his mind six times in the course of his studies, extending his college term by a solid two years, and it was hard to keep up.

Tossing the pillow to the ground, she leaned over and grabbed her phone from the charging station and set the alarm. This was completely unacceptable. Dean deserved a much better friend and she was determined to be one. She returned the device to its holder and snuggled down under the covers, pulling them up tight around her neck.

She held the ring-adorned hand close to her heart, where she unrealistically wished she could keep it.

Staying up to stare at pretty, sparkly things was a decision she regretted when the blaring alarm sounded out only a handful of hours later, but she switched it off and spun, planting her feet on the hardwood floor beside the bed. Her eyes barely open, she padded into the bathroom, stripped off her clothes, and let the hot spray work its magic to revitalize her as much as possible.

She toweled off and dressed, then tip-toed into the kitchen. Dean's light snores from the couch sent another wave of guilt crashing into her. His feet dangled over the armrest at the end of the sofa while she was completely dwarfed in his bed. Another thing he'd given her without question, his comfort for hers.

As quietly as possible she moved in his small kitchen, pulling together all the ingredients for a spinach and mushroom quiche, mildly impressed at how well Dean's refrigerator was stocked. But the small boxes of vegetarian sausage and plant-based chicken strips mixed in with Dean's staples of bacon and beef tugged at her heart.

In that moment she realized just how much she'd missed her best friend. Even though she'd grown incredibly close to Angela, one of the members of her team, over the years they'd traveled from one corner of the globe to the other, their bond wasn't the same as the one she had with Dean.

Inevitably when she was laying alone beneath the netting that covered her and her bed to keep mosquitos away, she'd have a twinge of homesickness that nearly always centered around the Carlisle family. A group of people she liked to claim as her own, even if there weren't any blood ties. She'd missed Dean like crazy, but the entire clan held a special place in her heart.

The same heart that shivered in her chest at the jolt of pain that came from the remembrance of her deception to those she loved most in the world.

Something she did for own family, even though Helena had never shown her even a fraction of the warmth Tracy Carlisle did.

Somehow she managed to mix together all the ingredients, fill the pan, and set it in the oven without her brain actually engaging in the task, too preoccupied with its current path of self-damnation. Questions about the decisions she made—and roped Dean into—threatened to drown her under their weight.

She was still distracted when a hand landed on her shoulder, making her jump two feet in the air and spin around, brandishing the spatula she held to serve the quiche like it was a weapon.

Dean laughed and held his hands up, palms out to her. "I promise I come in peace."

She smacked his bicep lightly, well, sort of lightly, and turned to silence the timer signaling the food was done cooking. "You don't do anything in peace. You have redefined 'troublemaker' since childhood and I have pictures as proof."

A look of mock panic crossed his face. "I thought you got rid of those."

"Nope." She popped the end of the word for emphasis. "A girl needs to be prepared." She gestured to the table already adorned with silverware, napkins, and two glasses of orange juice accompanied by a steaming mug of coffee for Dean and a cup of tea for her. "Sit down, this only has to set for a few minutes, then we can eat. You don't have to leave until eight, right?"

Dean's eyes tracked her movements and gave her inexplicable butterflies when she caught him staring at her out of the corner of her vision. *It's simply been too long*, she told herself. *That's the only reason I'm acting this way. It's just Dean, after all.*

He took a long draw from the coffee and inhaled deeply when she set the plate in front of him. "So Jillybean, to what do I owe the honor of this delicious meal?"

She shrugged and filled her own dish, taking the seat next to him. She had every intention of playing it off, but the cloud of deceit following her since her return was bothersome enough. "You've been amazing. I have asked the world of you and you've not only gone along with a ridiculous plan," she glanced down at her ring and stroked the inside of the band with her thumb, "but you've managed to go above and beyond. And meanwhile...I haven't asked one damn thing about you. How you've been, what's going on at the ranch, and what in the blue hell Mat is doing here."

90

She leaned forward and grabbed his forearm. "Please tell me that Mat actually is here and I wasn't hallucinating that entire thing in some weird hangover-induced stupor."

"No, he's real. He moved here permanently almost a year ago." Dean chuckled and pushed a forkful of the quiche in his mouth. The laughter dissolved into a moan of contentment. "Damn, this is phenomenal."

Heat worked its way up the column of her neck. "Thanks for the compliment, Sparky, but I still want answers."

His cell phone called out from the counter behind him and he leaned back in his seat to grab it. With an annoyed groan, he swiped several times across the screen before setting the device down next to him. He shoveled in the rest of his food in record time and stood up. "Shit, I'm running late."

He disappeared in that moment, and faster than she could blink he reappeared with a towel slung around his waist, his hair damp from a record breaking shower. "Breakfas wath amating," he garbled out around the foam and toothbrush hanging out of his mouth before vanishing again.

Dean emerged seconds later in a t-shirt and jeans. Disappointment swept over Jillian as he tugged his light jacket on and shoved his feet into a pair of tan boots. He caught her gaze from across the room and she noticed the lines forming around his lips. Even more questions than the unanswered ones that she'd already asked popped up in her mind.

A small smile that didn't quite reach his dark blue eyes curled his lips. "How about I bring home Chinese and we can binge watch whatever reality show you

91

need to get caught up on? We can talk more then." His expression moved from thinly veiled concern to goofy in seconds and he threw her a wink before opening the front door. "That's the kind of thing old married couples do on Friday nights anyway, right?"

Before she could answer, he vanished, softly latching the door closed behind him.

Chapter Ten

Dean

Thirteen Years Ago

"You're kidding with that shit, right?"

Dean grinned over at Jillian. "Mighty dirty mouth for a proper lady there, Miss Monroe. Must be the influence of a good man."

She rolled her eyes and splashed him with water as they trod in the pond that was far too small for any meaningful swimming. "First of all, we are fourteen. You can't call yourself a man at fourteen. Second of all...yes, it is completely all your fault."

He paddled a few short feet until his toes touched the grainy bottom and he walked the rest of the way to the edge, plopping down on the towel stretched across the rock and baking in the summer sun. "Come on, Jillybean, it'll be fun. Also, feel free to not mention to my mother all the words I've taught you over the years. She still yells at Tanner for swearing and he's an adult."

The reflected shine on the water made reading her

93

face impossible. "I don't know…"

"S'mores." He pulled out the biggest gun he had, her favorite dessert. The same one she'd never had until the ripe old age of ten when he'd first introduced her to the gooey creation that she immediately fell in love with. "We can roast hot dogs and make s'mores and I can tell you the most gruesome ghost story I can think of before I send you home to your bed in the glass castle."

Jillian groaned as she followed the same path he'd just taken and stretched out on the blanket beside him. It was weird seeing his best friend change and he wasn't sure he liked it. The skinny girl who'd made herself right at home in his world seven years ago was looking…different.

Sure all that makeup crap that her mother had caked on her face for certain functions made her look strangely untouchable, but even now when it was just the two of them hanging out by Fredrock and every single one of her freckles stood out, she wasn't the same.

Her long flame-colored hair glistened in the sun. She was still much shorter than him, but her small body was filling out in ways he couldn't help but notice. And he couldn't give her full lips more than a passing glance or thoughts about her would go to places they absolutely did not belong.

Jillian was beautiful.

He cleared his throat and stared off in the opposite direction. No matter what, this was still Jillian. She was his best friend, not a girl he should be looking at that way.

"I'd have to be back by midnight."

The smile returned to Dean's face. Damn, he loved

94

winning. "You know my mom gives me a curfew even when it's summer and even when I'm just in the backyard, so that isn't an issue."

She rotated her head and lifted a hand to shield her eyes from the sun. "You better make my s'mores right this time. The marshmallow has to be on fire before it's actually done."

He rolled his eyes and laid back on his towel beside her. "Don't worry, I know what to do."

Several minutes of silence stretched between them with only buzzing from a random passing dragonfly or bee to break the quiet. Before he was actually ready to move, Jillian stood and grabbed the clothes she'd worn to cover her swimsuit and began pulling them on.

"I need to go home and shower and at least pretend that I care what boring function my parents are going to tonight." She neatly folded the towel that he would throw directly in the dirty clothes bin as soon as he crossed the threshold of his house and twisted and tugged until her hair was in something that looked way too good to belong on a girl who just spent the past two hours swimming in a pond. "They're leaving around seven-thirty so I can just come around eight. Henry and Frieda don't care and they'll never breathe a word to my parents."

With a grumble he managed to keep contained in his brain, Dean rose to his feet, slung his towel over his shoulder, and shoved hers under his arm. "I'll wait for you by Fredrock. You don't need to walk all the way to my house by yourself. And you know my dad will insist on driving you home."

She took a few steps away, then turned back to him and bit her bottom lip and raised her hand, curling her

95

fingers in a small goodbye. She opened her mouth and closed it, then cleared her throat before speaking. "See you then."

He was almost certain he caught a glimpse of red on her cheeks he didn't think came from the sun.

Weird. Girls were just plain weird. The uneasy roll of his stomach made him wonder if weird was contagious.

***

Jillian

Thirteen Years Ago

"I'm perfectly capable of walking to your house by myself. You didn't have to stand there like some creeper watching me from the time I walked out the back door." Jillian crossed her arms and huffed as she stomped past where Dean was waiting by Fredrock, exactly as promised.

Dean shoved his hands in the front pockets of his denim shorts. "Even if I didn't want to make sure you were okay, my mom would've skinned me alive if I didn't. She harps on us all the time to be considerate and gentlemanly. Whatever the hell that means."

The corners of her stomach tickled from the butterfly wings a sudden bout of nerves created in her belly. Nerves? With Dean? She tried to ignore that and focus on her rapidly fading irritation with him. "Your mother is a saint to put up with you alone, much less all four of you."

"Hey," he nudged her shoulder as they crested the

small hill that brought his home into view, "I'm supposed to be your best friend. As in you have my back through thick or thin."

Jillian threw him a suspicious look in the slowly fading light of the late summer evening. "I thought you said you were making a bonfire."

With all the exaggerated drama only Dean could affect, he rolled his eyes and threw his hands up toward the sky before dropping them against his thighs. "I am going to make a fire." He pointed to a mound in the distance. "See, I have a stack of logs and branches ready to go."

She frowned as they closed in on the pile of wood. "Why didn't your dad already get it going? Or Wyatt or Tanner?"

He dipped his chin and zeroed in a lethal laser gaze. "Seriously? I mean...seriously? Jillybean, you've known me for seven years. Do you really think I need my dad or any of my brothers to build a fire for me?"

Jillian lifted one shoulder and surveyed the wooden structure in the center of a two foot tall ring of stone that reminded her of pictures she'd seen of teepees. She plopped down on one of the dozen Adirondack chairs situated around the pit. "I don't know what it takes. The fireplaces at my house are all gas, so my dad just pushes a button and they light up."

She bit back the giggle that threatened to spill out as he gathered some small twigs and two weird looking rocks, mumbling the entire time about the glass castle, his nickname for the cold, unwelcoming house she grew up in. She turned her head and gave a little sigh as she drank in the sprawling two story brick structure Dean called home. It was spacious, only slightly smaller than hers, but even from the outside it held a warmth she'd never experienced at her own place.

Glass castle was, sadly, a completely accurate nickname. Untouchable, uninviting, unfeeling.

A bright spark caught the corner of her eye and she whipped her head back around to face him. "What in the world are you doing?"

Dean looked up at her with a blatantly confused expression. "I'm starting a fire." He enunciated each word clearly and slowly. "What part of this doesn't make sense, Jillybean?" He lowered his head and returned to striking one stone against the other.

"Don't you need like a lighter or a match or something?" She fidgeted with the hem of her shorts romper, too afraid to blink for fear Dean's little experiment would wind up in him getting hurt. Freaking show off.

He grinned the same carefree, mischievous grin that most certainly always signaled trouble. "Watch and be amazed." He hit the rocks off each other a dozen more times and a spark caught onto the small pile of ground up something, causing it to smoke. He grabbed a few twigs from the pile and, with more care than she'd ever seen Dean Carlisle exhibit, stuck them in the middle of the gray column rising gracefully from what looked like nothing more than dirt and he gently blew into the billowing cloud. A flame appeared on the branches so quickly it seemed like magic.

Jillian's mouth fell open as he situated the fiery stick in the middle of the upright logs and repeated his actions two more times. Within minutes the small flickering grew into a small inferno. This boy somehow managed to create all this completely on his own.

Her awe quickly dissolved into irritation as she lifted her eyes and caught him standing beside the growing fire he'd built, hands on his hips and an arrogant smirk plastered across his face. "Proud of yourself there, Sparky?"

One thick, dark brow lifted and he looked down at her. "Um, Sparky?"

She drew her brows together and pursed her lips, dropping her voice an octave. "Boy make fire. Boy get new name. Boy now Sparky."

Dean rolled his eyes toward the rapidly dimming sky and plopped into the seat beside her. "You are such a dweeb, you know that, right?"

Jillian folded her hands across her abdomen and laid back in the chair. "You're the one who has a dweeb for a best friend. Don't you think that makes you the real loser here?"

Before he could respond, Connor appeared bearing a tray laden with hot dogs, buns, condiments, and, most importantly, all the ingredients for s'mores. Closely behind him, Michael and Tracy Carlisle followed with paper plates, glasses, and pitchers of lemonade and iced tea.

They ate and talked and laughed. It was easy, fun, and relaxing. And something Jillian could never get enough of. She knew that long before she was ready she'd return to her very privileged and very fortunate life, but one that lacked the connection and affection the Carlisles exuded effortlessly.

"Hey."

Dean's voice unceremoniously broke the spell she'd fallen under staring at the flames dancing in the fire pit and listening to the chatter around her. She turned her head toward him and blinked several times to bring his face into focus.

"You weren't serious about that whole Sparky thing, right?"

She grinned over at him. "Oh, I am beyond serious. For now and forever more you shall be my Sparky, maker of fire and chief Neanderthal."

He threw one of the marshmallows in her direction and she laughed, batting it away before it collided with her cheek. They both fell back into a comfortable silence, occasionally responding to something his parents said or, more often, Dean sending a well directed barb back in Connor's direction, usually resulting in both boys earning a scolding from their parents.

Jillian's eyes grew heavy as her full stomach and the hypnotizing flames lulled her into a blissful state of comfort. Voices of people she'd grown to love fell into nothing more than distant murmurs as sleep stole her away.

Deep down in a corner of her heart she never showed, she wished this crazy family that was sometimes a little too loud, always offered joking insults that were often accompanied with reckless dares, and that showed each member endless amounts of love and acceptance was hers.

Chapter Eleven

Dean

Present Day

"It's not funny." Jillian planted her hands on her hips and frowned.

Dean grabbed his midsection and doubled over, her irritation with him only fueling the waves of laughter rolling through him. "No, no, no." He tried to stand and wipe the tears from his eyes. "You're right, it isn't funny. It's damn hysterical."

She sighed, but the corners of her lips twitched with a repressed smile. "We're on a tight timeline here, Sparky. If it takes all day then it takes all day, but I have to pick colors and place settings and bridesmaid dresses and *my* dress..." Her gaze dropped to her feet. She crossed the small living room, angled one leg beneath her, and sat down on the couch. "It doesn't really matter anyway. I should just agree to whatever Mother thinks is best."

Once more, a sharp stab of pain pricked the edge of

his heart. She had no earthly clue how genuine his vows were going to be. The confession of his true feelings danced on the tip of his tongue, but he swallowed it down again. He hadn't a clue what the right time would look like or exactly what he was waiting for, but he had to hope in some magical sign. One that certainly wasn't presenting itself right now.

He took a seat beside her and searched for words that would be neutral, but as honest as possible. This was definitely not the moment he was waiting for. "Hey, it matters. It is irrelevant that this may be an unconventional wedding, what you want matters."

She turned slightly and buried her face in his shoulder, wrapping her arms around his waist and making his heart stop beating at the same time. "I'm so sorry, Dean. This is wholly unfair to you and I have zero right to bitch about something as stupid as a wedding dress for a fake wedding that—"

Dean pushed her away slightly. "Hey, first of all, you never call me Dean and I'm not entirely certain I like it." He ran a thumb beneath her left lower lid to catch the tear that spilled over the edge. "And second of all, regardless of what has led us to get married, you deserve to be happy and enjoy the day."

"So I should just pretend this is my actual wedding and not a day where I am manipulating my best friend into bailing my entire family out." Her eyes widened until they were saucers and she clamped a hand over her mouth.

Her entire family? Questions that he'd shoved to the back of his mind since she first made the insane proposition flooded forward again, but the look on her face made it pretty damn clear she wasn't letting anything slip. "Not ready to let that horse out of the barn yet, are you?"

"You've been working with Wyatt too long," she murmured from behind the fingers still pressed to her lips.

Dean rolled his eyes and released the hold he had on her bicep. "You know I won't push. Hell, you know I am the least pushy of all the Carlisle boys. Probably why everyone loves me the best." He threw her a wink that earned him a hefty sigh. "But it'd be nice if you could remember that I'm your best friend and would never spill any secrets. I never once breathed a word when you made out with—"

She put both hands against his mouth with a force that sent him backwards until he was laying on the cushions and she was straddling his midsection. Not a bad position to be in from his perspective, but still surprising. "Don't you dare finish that sentence, Dean Carlisle."

"I said I didn't tell anyone about that." His words came out jumbled even to his own ears as he spoke them against her palms.

For just a little longer than three beats of his racing heart, she sat still and stared down at him. Her firm grip eased and his breath hitched in his chest.

Now? Was this the *moment?* As soon as the question surfaced in his mind, she hopped off him, breaking the spell he hoped she felt as strongly as he did.

"Fine, but if I am going to be the monster bride, you have to as well." She propped her fists on her hips and straightened out to her full five foot one inch height. "That means you have to come to all the dinner samples and cake testing appointments that are lined up over the next few days."

Dean laced his fingers together behind his head and grinned at her. "Jillybean, you say that like it's some sort of punishment. You're telling me I get to have free food and cake? I hate to break it to ya, but that sounds like a great night out to me."

She lifted one brow and gave him a smile that managed to unsettle him and, oddly, excite him all at once. "But remember my mother will be there front and center because, trust me, Sparky, if we choose the chicken marsala, but she thinks the panko breaded chicken is a better option, you better believe that fight will be on."

He turned on the couch and rose to his feet. "The right kind of food can make me ignore everything. Even the Ice Queen's death glare and annoying voice."

Jillian folded her arms across her chest. The corners of her lips twitched with the laughter he knew she was holding in. No matter her mood, he could almost always draw out at least a giggle from her. "But will your brother let you free for all the millions of decision planning moments you need to be present for?"

Yeah, she would definitely think he needed to go to Wyatt for permission. He'd never actually told her... "Trust me, that's not an issue."

She tilted her head to the side and narrowed her eyes. "What do you do there, anyway, Sparky? I can't really picture you mucking out stalls all day." She poked him in the ribcage. "But after your third major change, maybe you picked that instead."

"Don't worry that pretty little head, Jillybean. I will be there with bells on for any and every decision I need to give my expert and desperately needed opinion on."

104

The mental list of the things he needed to tell her had another bullet point labeled "career" added to it. Right below the bright, glaring, blinking red "tell her you love her" that held the number one spot.

***

Jillian

Present Day

The third lace gown her mother had picked for her itched more than the previous two. It was the very last thing she'd ever pick out for herself, but as she had with so many other details, she mostly let her mother have free rein, although listening to the complaints about buying off the rack because of the tight timeline nearly sent her over the edge. And definitely drove her to remind her mother, once again, the role she played in everything that led to making this necessary.

Helena Monroe had actually managed to shut up for an entire five minutes. Damn near miraculous.

Despite her silent assertions that she absolutely would not wear the latest dress her mother had chosen, she exited the changing room with the attendant in tow to fluff out the chapel length train. She stepped up on the platform surrounded by full-length mirrors on three sides to the ooh's and ahh's of her bridal party—the daughters of her mother's friends, not anyone Jillian actually hung out with.

What she wouldn't give to have Angela sitting there instead of the three nearly identical, perfectly coifed heads. Not only because she adored her friend, but because Angela would undoubtedly be sporting khaki shorts and an olive tank top. Practical when they were working in the field, but a wardrobe staple for the other woman that would drive her mother into an apoplectic fit.

Instead of someone she loved standing by her side, her attendants were hand chosen by Helena and fit the social ideal the mother required.

Ainsley, Presley, and Bridget had been acquaintances in school and girls she'd given small, congenial smiles to at social functions they'd all been required to attend, but there was a glaring difference between them and Jillian. They all were cookie cutter copies of their own mothers, happy to gossip about who was seen with who at a garden party supposedly organized to raise money to build wells in Africa, but really were designed to rub elbows with all the right people.

And talk about all the wrong ones.

Jillian turned dutifully on the pedestal and frowned at her reflection. Nope. Not happening. "I hate it," she declared as she hefted the skirt and stepped onto the carpeted floor. As she crossed to the dressing room to rid herself of the itchy material she was brought to a stop by one of the gowns hanging.

Ivory colored satin immediately caught her eye and she asked the clerk if she could see the full gown, but when the assistant helping her in and out of the various fluffy confections pulled the dress free from between others, Jillian had the feeling of perfection she'd heard described on the trash reality shows she forced Dean to watch with her. Simple, elegant, and timeless. The exact dream gown she never actually knew she wanted until she saw it.

She caught the arm of the girl who was probably the same age as her. "I want to try that on."

The bateau neckline led to fitted sleeves that ended just below the elbow. A thin line of identical satin ribbon cinched the waist and the material curved to hug her hips before flaring into a trumpet skirt with a train just slightly longer than the chapel length one she'd just worn.

"This is it."

She breathed out the words so softly the worker leaned in closer and asked her to repeat herself. "This is the one." This time her voice reflected the confidence she felt in making the proclamation.

The decision was cemented by the silence as she stepped from the back room. Every member of her bridal party sat with mouths agape until they simultaneously erupted in squeals and giggles and nods of approval.

All except Helena, who coldly glared at her from across the room as she stood on the elevated surface. Jillian lifted her chin in spite of the clear disapproval that managed to make her feel five years old again. And like an impossible failure.

Until the older clerk discreetly walked over to her mother and whispered something in her ear that made Helena visibly brighten and actually smile.

"What did she say?" She couldn't hold back the question as she sat beside her mother in the backseat of the town car as they rode back to her house.

Helena jolted slightly as if Jillian's words had pulled her from a trance. "Excuse me?"

Jillian fiddled with the hem of her emerald tunic top.

"At the bridal store you weren't very happy with my gown until the owner said something to you. What did she say?"

Her mother lifted a finely sculpted brow slightly. "You chose a wonderful designer, darling. The same one several celebrities have used. Very well done." Helena turned down the corners of her mouth. "Although they certainly weren't buying off the rack."

Jillian barely stifled the groan threatening to explode. Naturally, her mother wasn't happy that she loved the dress. She didn't smile because she thought her daughter looked beautiful. It was all smoke, mirrors, and appearance. She turned to face the window and stared out at the slowly setting sun.

She tracked every mile they traveled that brought her closer to the townhouse she was sharing with Dean. A warm wave of comfort washed over her. It felt like home. So much more than the massive house she grew up in. Her fingers fell to the silver handle before the driver had even pulled to a complete stop. She was certain her mother would be disappointed that she hadn't waited for the driver to open it for her.

"Have a nice evening, Mother." She climbed out of the car as soon as it was thrown into park and barely stopped herself from racing up the cement steps to the front door.

The exhaustion of the day hit her hard as she turned the handle and crossed the threshold. All she could think about was finding the nearest horizontal surface and passing out for some yet-to-be-determined period of time.

Until the decadent scent of basil, oregano, and tomatoes tickled her nose and drew her into the kitchen.

The rich aromatic smells triggered her stomach to growl. Inquiries as to exactly what Dean was cooking and pleas to have even a small sample if it wasn't yet ready all died on her tongue when he came into full view.

"You have *got* to be kidding me."

Dean turned and offered a dazzling smile for a full second before it disappeared. "What? You don't like stuffed shells now? It's a meatless sauce." He hefted a pot over to the counter and ladled out some of the self-proclaimed vegetarian tomato sauce onto the baking dish sitting beside it.

She crossed the few feet separating them and stood next to him with a small, but wholly intentional, bump of her hip on his. "You know it's one of my favorites and I'll be damned if that doesn't smell like Izzy's sauce, but I'm talking about the outfit there, Sparky. 'I cook as good as I look?'"

After a quick glance down at the apron he was sporting, he gave her a completely unrepentant grin. "Hey, I don't need any splatter getting on my clothes." He shrugged and lined up the already filled pasta shells on the glass dish with intense precision. "Besides, don't women love a man who brings home the bacon and cooks it? Well, fake bacon for you. Although we probably should discuss that topic soon because I'm not certain I'm willing to give up my bachelorhood and bacon at the same time."

Jillian shook her head, but couldn't fight the smile that popped up. "How do you do that?"

Dean drew his brows together as he spread more sauce over the top of the shells and sprinkled mozzarella cheese on top of that. "Do what? Make dinner?"

She tilted her head and rested it against his bicep with a small sigh. "No, how do you manage to make me smile and forget the fact that I had a perfectly shitty day in less than five minutes?"

He stiffened slightly beside her before putting one arm around her waist and squeezing slightly. "Isn't that what a good husband would do?"

His hand fell away and he moved to set the heaping dish in the oven already radiating warmth in the small space. Jillian turned and rested her hip against the counter, tracking Dean's motions.

Exactly when had her best friend stopped being immature and irresponsible and how had she never noticed? She could blame her infrequent visits home and sporadic Skype chats, but a good friend would still manage to see these things.

And a good friend especially would know what he did at Wyatt's ranch.

While she'd been lost in her own head, Dean managed to pour her a large glass of chardonnay. "How about you tell me about your shitty day while this cooks?"

She took the proffered, and much needed, adult beverage and took a long swing. "Only if you tell me how work was, Sparky."

He lifted his own glass and tapped it against hers with a grin. "Deal."

Chapter Twelve

Dean

Thirteen Years Ago

"Did you run here in *that*?" Dean skidded his bike to a halt and dropped it to the ground beside the lake just as Jillian reached him, her chest heaving under the beaded emerald dress.

She hefted the material and plopped onto the rock. "Shut up." She folded her arms across her front and huffed. After a handful of moments she hopped off the stone and began pacing, not missing a step on the uneven surface despite her two inch heels. "I am so over it."

Dean lifted his brows, but he knew his best friend and kept his mouth shut. She'd talk when she was ready. His eyes tracked her as he moved to take the seat she'd just abandoned. He flattened his palms against the warm stone slightly behind him and waited while she fumed.

Seconds became minutes as she huffed and snarled

and started to speak before dissolving into a frustrated growl and resuming her cadence.

Finally his impatience won out and he took off his baseball hat to wipe away the sweat beads that had formed as he pedaled to their meeting spot after her frantic and frustrated text that she wanted to see him. "Out with it."

His words had the miraculous effect to bring her steps to a halt. She stood as rigid as the trees surrounding them, her arms ramrod straight by her sides.

Her jaw flexed a few times before she pointed a condemning finger toward the house in the distance. "Her."

He raised one of his legs up to an angle and rested his forearm on his knee. "Yeah, I figured that. Only the Ice Queen can manage to rile you up like this." He tilted his head and watched as she started pacing again. "What did she do this time?"

Jillian gripped each elbow with the opposite hand and continued walking in a large oval. "Nothing. Everything. Just the same exact things she always does." She stopped and turned to him, the corners of her eyes filling with tears. "She uses posters of people starving and children begging for food as *selling points* to make the auction hit whatever number she has in her head as a win for the night."

She crossed the ground and sat down beside him, the frilly, fluffy skirt of the dress brushing against his leg, bare beneath his shorts.

He wanted to say the right thing, but didn't have the first clue what that was. Instead he pulled a long stalk of grass free from the small patch growing beside him and stuck it in his mouth.

"She is exploiting the people she receives constant and excessive praise for helping...and it isn't even actual help. She throws money at random organizations. She never checks them out to see if they are legitimate and actually send the money where it's supposed to go." Jillian pulled at pins and elastic bands until soft, ginger waves fell around her shoulders. "My mother is constantly presenting herself as an altruistic humanitarian, but only as much as it will look good, not do good."

Dean twisted his lips to the side. "I know it drives you crazy, but your mother has been a self-centered, social climbing witch since the dawn of time." He held up a hand. "Uh, no offense."

Jillian stared out on the horizon for several moments in silence. "I can't have a life like hers, Dean."

When she used his real name instead of the nickname she'd given him, he knew to pay attention. "You're nothing like her."

Her hand swept up and down to encompass the designer gown he couldn't even begin to guess the cost of. "Aren't I? I'm sitting here in a designer gown bitching"—her eyes darted around as soon as the curse slipped from her lips and it made Dean grin—"about her being privileged, but I am really any better?"

"You see an issue with it. She doesn't." He lifted a shoulder and shifted uncomfortably on the rock. He was fourteen, what the hell did he know about poverty, wealth, need, or social status? "I think that makes you better."

His parents might be something more than comfortable now, but they didn't let much time go between reminders to their boys that it hadn't always been that way for them and they expected their sons to work hard for everything they got, not skate by because their family had built a successful company. That, however, was the extent of his fiscal knowledge.

And although his parents had often preached kindness, empathy, and giving back, he knew jack shit about the kind of charities her mother worked with. All of those reasons equaled out to him keeping his mouth shut aside from agreeing with Jillian and letting her vent out all the emotions he knew she kept locked tightly away while she put on the performance of being the dutiful daughter.

"I want my life to mean something."

Her simple statement cut through the confusing thoughts clouding his brain and brought his head up from where it had been bent, examining his sneakers.

He pulled his brows together. "What the hell does that mean? Your life means a lot."

The gentle shake of her head sent a soft waterfall of red waves over her shoulder. When had her hair gotten so long? "No, I want it to mean something. I want to go to Ethiopia and Bolivia and Honduras and…everywhere there is a need." She grabbed his hands and held them tightly in hers, her green eyes glowing with something he couldn't recognize, but something that made his heart jump a few beats. "I want to physically help the people who need it the most, not just throw enough money at a cause to make myself sleep better at night and look like a hero to my friends."

The passion in her voice was contagious. "You can do anything you want, Jillybean." And at that moment in time he had never believed more in a single statement.

***

Jillian

Thirteen Years Earlier

Tap, tap, tap.

Jillian groaned and rolled over. It was a Saturday and she was determined to sleep in.

Tap, tap, tap.

Her groan turned into a growl as she threw back the covers and planted her feet on the floor. She padded to the door and yanked it open just as the obnoxious offender on the other side had lifted their hand to knock again.

"Sparky?" She yawned and scratched the head of hair she was certain had twisted into a giant rat's nest overnight... as always. "What the hell are you doing here this early?"

As soon as she said the word she grabbed his wrist and pulled him into her room. She stuck her head out of the doorway long enough to glance up and down the hall before shutting the door and her eyes in unison and sagging against it.

Dean chuckled in response to her momentary panic and she rewarded it with a glare. "You certainly have developed quite the potty mouth there, Ms. Monroe."

She shoved him as she walked past to bury herself beneath her covers again. "It's all thanks to your horrendous influence on my vocabulary, Mr. Carlisle. Now you can feel free to tell me why you're bothering me early on a Saturday morning, how you got in here, and then you can leave."

"Frieda loves me. Your mother is at a garden party. It's nearly eleven. And I have plans for you. So stop whining and get yourself out of bed." He tugged at the covers and grinned at her grimace as the light hit her face again. "It would be preferable for you to shower and dress, but I'm not opposed to dragging you out of here in your pajamas."

She pressed her lips together and rolled her eyes, begrudgingly sitting up once more. "As if you're strong enough."

Dean lifted the short sleeves of his t-shirt and flexed his lanky arms into surprising baby muscles. "Wanna try it?"

"Ugh." She stood beside the bed and stretched for a minute before crossing the room to her walk-in closet and rummaging around for clothes. "I don't have the energy to fight you. You're lucky this time. Casual, I presume, since that's all your wardrobe consists of."

He stopped playing with the bottles lining her vanity and whipped his head toward her. "Hey, I resemble that remark."

Jillian grabbed her clothes and headed to the *en suite*. "Give me fifteen. You can feel free to give yourself a makeover if you're that interested in my makeup."

She closed the door with a soft click...and flicked the lock. Their easy friendship sometimes didn't feel quite as easy as it used to before they became teenagers. She raced through her shower, sprayed unhealthy amounts of detangler in her hair and wrangled her wavy locks into something resembling a ponytail, though not the sleek one she wished she could pull off, and managed to emerge from the bathroom with thirty seconds to spare.

"I'm kinda disappointed you aren't rocking that cotton candy lip gloss."

Dean rolled his eyes and stood from the small stool that sat in front of her vanity. "If her highness is ready, our chariot is waiting. And by chariot, I mean truck. Driven by Wyatt, so there is a high likelihood that the smell of horses and hay and I don't even want to imagine what else could very well become imbedded in your clothes."

She looked down at her romper and sandals then back at him and shrugged. "Risk I'm willing to take, I guess. Lead on, Sir Sparky."

The ride was exactly how Jillian knew it would be. She sat on the bench seat, scrunched between Dean and Wyatt, not only physically but verbally as the two sparred the entire drive. Lost in the headache-inducing bickering that was so common to the brothers, she paid zero attention to their destination until Dean pulled her out of the car, barking at his brother over his shoulder to come back in a few hours.

"Dean..." Even she could hear all the caution that was twining her stomach into knots pour into her tone.

He gripped her shoulders and turned her to face him. "You aren't her. You have more compassion and empathy in your little finger than she has in her whole body."

A small jolt ran through her. "Wow, Dean...that's deep. Especially for you."

He dipped his head, crimson staining his cheeks. "I heard Mom say something like that to my aunt once and it seemed to really make her happy."

Naturally, Dean hadn't thought of that himself. Her gaze found its way back to the weathered sign on the front of the building showing minor signs of aging, Harrold Memorial Homeless Shelter. But he had thought of this, thought of her, and that meant the world.

In a rare moment of foresight she would have never believed Dean capable of, he had apparently called ahead and spoken with someone about their arrival because two staff members greeted them as soon as they pushed through the glass front door. They both spent the next several hours working side-by-side to fill backpacks with water bottles, crackers, beef jerky, tissues, and hygiene supplies.

The statistics the workers easily rattled off about the number of men, women, and most heartbreaking to her, children that lived on the streets gnawed a hole in her gut at the same time as it reaffirmed her desire to work to make even a tiny difference in the world. Even if that meant only one person.

Dean hadn't said much as they worked together, but as they sat beside each other on the cement steps that led into the building waiting for Wyatt's return, he tilted his head a little and looked at her. "She would never have done anything even remotely like that."

Jillian laid her head on his shoulder. "Thanks, Sparky. For...for everything."

118

Chapter Thirteen

Dean

Present Day

Dean slid his hand in the one the younger man had stuck out at the end of their session and gave it a firm shake as well as offering an encouraging smile. "You're doing great, Chase. Even before Mat shared your progress with me, I could tell you were making a positive change. You should be proud of yourself."

His cousin appeared on his left and leaned against the railing that kept the horses corralled in the paddock. "Me too," his cousin agreed with a nod.

Chase dropped his head and released his grip, rubbing the back of his neck. "Thanks. I...feel better. Clearer. I have a focus that I don't remember ever having before." He looked off into the cloudless crystal sky for a moment then turned his gaze on Mat. "It still isn't easy though."

"And it may never be. It should get easier as time goes on and you develop new skills and techniques, but it may never be easy." Mat shook his head. "But you're gaining ways to cope with cravings or triggers to get through the harder spots."

Chase turned back to the chestnut horse he'd been working with that day who was trotting along the far perimeter of the enclosure and a grin spread across his face. "Yeah, I am." A burgundy sedan slowly appeared on the crest of the driveway, headed toward where the three men stood. "That's my ride. Gotta go. See you guys in a couple of days."

With that, the younger man ducked between two of the wooden rails and jogged off to meet the vehicle just as it pulled to a stop.

Dean stared at Chase's retreating back for several moments before facing his cousin again. "Witnessing that kind of turnaround never gets old."

Mat pressed his lips together in a thin line, the five years and copious amounts of additional experience he had on Dean deepening the fine lines around his eyes. "Not every story is a success story."

Just as Dean opened his mouth to respond, Wyatt emerged from the barn, an obnoxious swagger to his step that he'd always possessed, but somehow seemed to worsen with each passing day. Either that or Dean was just annoyed at being confronted with it so often.

"Well, well, well, if it isn't my two favorite ranch hands in one place." A familiar barb, but one that never failed to incite Dean to roll his eyes in response.

Correcting Wyatt was futile and would likely only make his brother continue the prodding. He knew that deep down, Wyatt loved the unique dynamic that Mat and Dean's project, their baby, brought to the ranch. He proved that when he let the two take the chance of starting it at RA Ranch, the dream Wyatt had long held that he finally brought to fruition a few years earlier.

Of course, having Georgia strongly on their side and more than happy to push her husband to agree to the plan didn't hurt either.

But his older brother could still be useful. And, dammit all to hell he hated to admit it, but he needed Wyatt's advice. "Hey Wy, got a second?"

Wyatt turned down the corners of his mouth and drew his brows together. "Everything okay?"

Mat pulled a slightly dusty baseball cap from his back pocket and adjusted the brim before plopping it on his head. He gestured to the horse Chase had been working with and took a few steps in that direction. "I'm gonna take Ginger back in and give her a few apples for being so good today."

As soon as their cousin was on the other side of the pen and had the horse's reins in his hands, Wyatt rested a booted foot on the bottom rail and his forearms on the top one. He stared at Dean for several long moments in silence, the shadow from the brim of his cowboy hat doing nothing to lessen the intensity of his gaze.

"I need..." the word lodged in Dean's throat and he swallowed several times before saying it out loud, "...advice." Well used to all three of his older brothers dispensing unwanted opinions on everything from his career to his love life and even his wardrobe, Dean was fairly certain this was the first time he'd actually requested input.

In nearly any other circumstance he'd be turning to Connor. The two youngest members of the Carlisle clan had a unique bond that was forged from battling against their two older brothers as kids. But Wyatt was here and

121

he had certainly screwed up enough in his own relationship to be experienced enough to offer the insight Dean needed.

Wyatt snorted lightly. "That isn't very reassuring there, little brother. You basically never give a shit what anyone thinks. This has to be big."

Pulling the baseball cap off his head, Dean carded his fingers through his hair before putting the hat firmly back in place. "I'm just gonna rip the Band-Aid off here." He pointed at his brother with a firm note in his voice. "And this is top secret information here, Wy. Mom and Dad don't know. Tanner and Connor don't know. Hell, no one other than Jillian, her parents, myself, and probably some lawyer somewhere know this little tidbit and I want to keep it that way, got it?"

"Listen, whatever the hell it is isn't going anywhere beyond you and me, but you need to spill the beans after that disclaimer." He tilted his head to the side. "Are Jillian's parents pushing some kind of prenup or something?"

Dean gave a half huff, half laugh. "A prenup would be a gift compared to reality." He squared his shoulders and sucked in a deep lungful of air, hoping he chose the right brother to be his ally in what was possibly the most ridiculous scenario he could ever imagine. "Jillian and I, the engagement, the wedding, the whole damn thing it's…it's not real."

Wyatt squinted his blue eyes, identical to Dean's, disbelief etched on his face. "It looks pretty damn real to me. I've had lots of scans on damn near every part of my body including my head thanks to more throws from bulls than I care to remember and they've yet to find any brain trauma so unless this is some weird

122

voodoo bullshit, this is most definitely real."

Dean kicked his boots in the dusty ground. "I mean the actual relationship. Me and Jillian, being in love...the whole thing is fake." He swallowed down the boulder in his throat. "For her at least."

"You're gonna have to back up about a thousand paces and fill in the blanks. How the hell is this not real?"

Dean ran his tongue along the back of his teeth. "Jillian's in a tough spot. Hell, she hasn't really even told me why, which is pretty damn annoying, but she needed my help and that help happened to come in the form of an inheritance her grandfather left her." He took a deep breath. "And it can only be accessed after she gets married and *stays* married for eighteen months."

"But Jillian's family is loaded, why the hell would she need money?" Wyatt kicked a chunk of mud off his boot, shaking his head. "And is that kind of a requirement even legal? I mean, I could see that happening a few hundred years ago, but today?"

"Listen, I have no idea." Dean held both hands up, palms out toward his brother. "All I know is what she's willing to tell me and that hasn't been a hell of a lot. I'm the only person she says she could trust with this, which should make me feel as good as I can, given the circumstances."

"But?"

Dean quirked his lips to the side and glared at his brother. "But you assholes are right. Somehow I wound up falling in love with my best friend and pretending to be okay with this being some fake bullshit when..." He trailed off into a string of curses as Wyatt chuckled beside him. "It isn't funny."

His obnoxious older brother wiped a probably fictitious tear from his eye. "No, you're right. It isn't funny, it's frickin' hysterical."

He delivered a punch to Wyatt's bicep that was slightly more than playful. "Shut up. I need," the word burned his tongue even just thinking of it, "help."

A wide grin curled his brother's lips. "You've come to the right place, brother."

***

Jillian

Present Day

The seamstress made a final tuck near her feet and Jillian gratefully stepped from the elevated platform. The silence in the shop at her final fitting was like a gift and she reveled in changing back into her white capris and paisley top in peace. Her mother was far too consumed with floral arrangements, place settings, and a dozen other things Jillian couldn't care less about.

If this were her real wedding, her mother would be as far removed from it as Jillian could get her. But it wasn't. It was a legal contract only occurring to fulfill the requirements of another legal contract.

When her mother even so much as breathed the suggestion of implementing a prenup, Jillian had firmly and decisively planted her size six in the ground and refused to bring it up to Dean. She was already sinking beneath the weight of the guilt not only from simply asking him for this monumental favor, but for keeping the actual reason why it was so important from him as

124

well.

She didn't doubt for a moment that he would follow through with this, but an unusual measure of embarrassment at admitting the truth kept her mouth sealed shut.

The conflicting and confusing emotions she'd found herself mired in since her mother's first frantic phone call two months ago only deepened with the reminder that she'd dragged Dean into this and he'd been a freaking saint about the entire thing.

That was a title she never thought she'd bestow on him.

Her phone dinged and his name flashed across the screen along with a ridiculously goofy picture of the two of them that was taken just before she left for her most recent trip.

Dean: If my blushing bride is finished, I'll be there to pick her up in 15 minutes.

She rolled her eyes at the "blushing bride" bit, but couldn't stop the grin from taking over her face as she hastily typed out a reply. She'd just finished going over final details with the seamstress when a roaring engine came to a stop outside the glass door of the bridal shop. Seconds later Dean strolled in all swagger and bullshit, just like always.

"There's my beautiful wife-to-be." He smiled broadly, tossing a wink at the older woman behind the counter. "Ready to hit the road, sweet cheeks?"

Jillian kept her face as jovial as she knew it should be and allowed him to tuck her under his arm until they were on the sidewalk, the door softly swishing shut behind them. Then she smacked the back of her hand on his t-shirt clad chest and turned to him. "Sweet cheeks? Seriously, Sparky, that's what you came up with, sweet cheeks?"

Dean merely laughed in response and handed her a black full face helmet with a tinted sun shield. "How about you just put this on or I'll figure out something less adorable to call you, my darling wife?"

Her eyes bounced from the sleek motorcycle parked beside the curb to the helmet and then up to Dean several times in that order. "I am not getting on that thing with you."

"Aw, come on, Jillybean." He turned his mouth down into a pout that shouldn't be as adorable as it was. "I've even gotten Mom to ride with me. I promise I'll be extra safe. I wouldn't want anything to keep you from walking down the aisle with full use of all appendages."

She trapped her bottom lip between her teeth and rolled the helmet between her palms. "Nothing over forty." At the immediate brightening of his face, she held up one finger. "Make that thirty-five."

Dean threw one leg over the bike and patted the seat behind him before sliding his own, identical helmet in place. "You won't regret this. In fact, I'm pretty damn sure you're gonna love it. How many times did I take you on a ride when we were kids?"

With a snort she pulled the heavy hunk of plastic over her head, not fully convinced it could actually save her life in the event of a massive crash. She flipped up the visor so she could see well enough to take her place behind Dean and immediately wrapped her arms around his waist, not trusting her balance. "We weren't on major roads and we sure as hell weren't going at a speed that could get us maimed or worse."

He kicked the stand and planted both feet to hold the bike upright. She slid the tinted shield back in place and was amazed by the clear view, completely protected from the sun's bright rays. He revved the engine to life and she tightened her hold with a small "eep."

Somehow his deep voice spoke softly in her ears louder than the roaring machine. "Put your right hand up beside the visor, do you feel a small button there? Tap your index finger on my stomach twice if you find it."

Jillian felt around the plastic until she located the smooth circle and thumped her finger on the soft cotton covering his surprisingly firm abdomen. When had Dean grown a six pack?

"Good." The measured tone was gentle and managed to ensnare her already tangled stomach in a fresh knot, this one very different from the stress-induced ones she'd almost grown accustomed to. "If you press that you can talk to me through the Bluetooth mic in the facemask just like I'm talking to you now."

With that instruction, he kicked the bike into gear and sped off down the road. Jillian immediately returned her arm to his waist and held on tight, pressing her body firmly against his back. When they made a left turn onto a main road, she lifted a shaky hand to the button he'd told her about. "This feels like a lot faster than thirty-five, Sparky."

His answering laugh filled the helmet and the familiar sound managed to settle her nerves. "Trust me, Jillybean. I'd never let anything happen to you. Just relax and hold on tight."

With the simple reminder that of anyone in the world, she could trust him, some of the tension drained from her spine. As their ride progressed she practically melted into him, falling in love with the fresh air circling around her body and the countryside seemingly flying past.

He was absolutely right. This was amazing.

Right up until soft drops of rain soaked through her shirt and quickly grew to hard pelting drops that bit into her skin.

Once more Dean's voice came through the speaker and filled the space around her, first with a string of epithets. "I'm going to pull over up there a little bit. We can wait under the tree for this to pass."

Even though the large oak was just a couple of hundred feet ahead, the sudden cloud burst dumped buckets of water on them both, thoroughly soaking her light top. By the time they parked, she was shivering behind him.

He helped her off the bike and pressed her against the trunk of the tree. "I've got something for you."

Jillian's teeth chattered as she stood with her back on the roughened bark, hugging herself tightly. Even if she caught pneumonia it would be totally worth it. That was the most fun she'd had in longer than she cared to admit.

Dean pulled her close to him and dropped a heavy jacket around her shoulders, tugging it together, and bringing near immediate warmth. He cupped her cheek and he tilted her head up to look at him. "Better?"

She swallowed a few times, her voice failing every time she tried to speak so she finally simply nodded in response.

His hand stayed pressed to her face, his thumb slowly stroking across her damp skin, his eyes never once leaving hers. "Jilly...I..."

His words died off as his lips connected with hers. Shock melted into a warmth far more consuming than the leather coat offered. Her arms fell from being wrapped around her own side to move hesitantly around his waist.

The deep groan in the back of his throat vibrated against her and he pushed her slightly until her back was once again pressed to the solid trunk of the massive tree. His mouth moved over hers with a mixture of reverence and passion she had never expected Dean Carlisle to be capable of.

Dean. This was Dean. Her best friend since childhood. The keeper of too many of her secrets and now the white knight she never knew she needed.

And she was *kissing* him.

He pulled back, breaking the magic that blanketed them in the moment.

Nearly.

His labored breathing matched hers. "I'm sorry. I-I didn't...Jilly, this wasn't part of the plan."

An unusual wave of disregard swept over her. "Plans can change, can't they?" She snaked a hand up to the back of his neck, pulling his mouth toward hers once more. When a breath separated their lips she whispered, "Just for right now," before losing herself in the kiss she didn't know she wanted.

Chapter Fourteen

Dean

Twelve Years Earlier

"Hey, Mom, Jilly's coming over later."

Tracy Carlisle rolled her eyes at her son. "Hey, Mom, do you mind if Jillian comes over later?"

Dean frowned at his mother. "Same difference." He shrugged and tossed the football he was carrying in the air. "You love it when she comes over more than I do."

His mother stepped out from behind the kitchen island and grabbed the ball mid-air. "I do, but that doesn't mean you don't need to ask." She lifted her brows meaningfully at him and lowered her chin. "Understand?"

He grinned and stole the ball back from his mother with a wink. "Yes, ma'am." He turned to walk out the sliding glass door at the back of the house, but stopped and faced her again. "So...can she?"

She pressed her lips together in a thin line and nodded. "Of course she can."

With a quick glance around to make sure Connor wasn't hanging around to catch him in the rare moment of affection, he dropped a quick kiss on his mother's cheek and dashed out the back door. In completely predictable Connor fashion, Dean found his older brother outside with an array of pencils that looked to him to be identical, but that Connor insisted were all very different, and a large sketchpad.

Connor glanced up long enough to see Dean descend the tall wooden steps that led from the expansive deck to the backyard before returning his focus to the paper laid out before him.

Dean stood in front of his brother, blocking his view of whatever the hell it was that he was drawing and volleyed the football back and forth between his hands. "Wanna play?"

With a small lift to one brow, Connor looked up and gave a curt shake of his head. "Not right now."

He'd known it was a long shot. Connor was, by far, the least interested in any sport, unless you counted running as a sport, but with Tanner at college and Wyatt out who the hell knew where doing who the hell knew what, Connor was it by default. The close bond they shared may have meant they were each other's confidant and closest friends, but it didn't feed Dean's moderately competitive nature.

"Come on." He knew he was whining and he knew it was obnoxious, but he honestly didn't care. "Just fifteen minutes. Or ten. The trees or the grass or whatever it is you're drawing to get all the ooh's and ahh's from Mom and Aunt Sharon and the rest of your fan club will still be there."

If it wouldn't ruin the dynamic of good natured

bickering, Dean would admit out loud his silent admiration for the inherent talent his brother possessed.

At Connor's responding silence, Dean kicked at his foot a little. "Seriously, Jillybean is going to be coming over soon and she'll want to watch that stupid reality show and I'll be stuck inside for hours. Please, just a few minutes."

Connor set his art supplies on the Adirondack chair next to the one where he sat and sighed. "I'll compromise with you. I haven't gone for a run yet. Go with me and I'll knock my normal five miles down to just a mile and a half to compensate for your lazy ass."

Dean glanced up at the still closed glass patio door. "Awfully ballsy to use that kind of language where Mom could hear, but it's a deal as long as I get a raincheck for football soon."

"You're a fine one to talk, you've contaminated poor Jillian with your potty mouth." Connor stood and stretched to his full six foot height, a fact that slightly annoyed Dean, who was still a good five inches shorter. "Let me run and change my shoes and I'll meet you out front."

The two ran at a moderate pace that still allowed them to talk and trade barbs, but were fast enough they managed to get back to the Carlisle home just as Jillian walked up to the front door.

She lifted a perfectly manicured brow as the brothers approached. "Don't you two look...athletic."

Dean sucked in deep lungfuls of air. "Is that your hoity-toity way of saying we're sweaty, disgusting pigs?"

Jillian scrunched up her chin and jutted out her lower lip slightly. "It's called being polite, Sparky. You could try it once in a while."

Pushing past her with an exaggerated bump of his hip into hers, he opened the front door and headed toward the stairs. "I'll go…freshen up so I don't offend you. Go ahead and cue up all the drama while you wait. Feel free to make me a sandwich while you're at it."

He added the last bit as he jogged up the steps and was fairly certain that, as long as his mother was still in the kitchen, Jillian was flipping him off behind his back. And just the mental image brought an immediate grin to his face.

***

Jillian

Twelve Years Earlier

"You forgot the popcorn, loser."

Dean sighed and dropped down onto the couch beside her, passing a bottle of root beer. "We literally just had dinner twenty minutes ago. You can't possibly be hungry."

She turned to him, dipped her chin, and gave a hard stare. "Do you even know me?"

Grumbling just loud enough she could hear, but too low to make out the words, he stood and stomped off into the kitchen as she queued up the first of the three episodes remaining for their binge session. She snuggled deeper into the soft cushion, wishing her mother could value comfort over appearance with their furniture. None of it was even remotely plush enough to handle the hours she and Dean would sit watching their reality TV guilty pleasure.

Well, actually her guilty pleasure. Luckily, Dean was amused by the head-over-heels after one meeting insta-love the show was notorious for displaying. And he really enjoyed making fun of the guys she'd swoon over as they shyly offered a rose to the lucky winner.

Within a few minutes Dean returned with a heaping bowl of popcorn and a much smaller one of chocolate candy because he knew she loved to munch on the sweet and salty combination.

"You know you could've started without me." He plopped down beside her and grinned. "It takes a few minutes for one of the girls to start crying or the dude to be a royal asshole."

Jillian smacked the back of her hand against his chest. "Your mother might hear you." She popped a few kernels in her mouth along with some of the chocolate, the blending of the two almost pure bliss. "Besides you need to be quiet so I can pay attention to who gets the one-on-one date. Ugh. I really hope it isn't Rebecca. She is such an annoying know-it-all."

"Nah, she and Dad went out grocery shopping. Me and my potty mouth are safe." Dean rolled his eyes but stayed silent through the first two episodes.

Mostly.

"He's a bad kisser."

The comment laced with a note of grumpiness brought her attention from the screen to the boy sitting beside her. "Oh like you're some expert?" Laughter bubbled up inside her. "You've been on, what, a grand total of five whole dates but you're gonna compete with a thirty-year-old man?"

Dean chuckled and took a long draw from the glass

134

bottle of soda. "Jillybean, dates aren't the only times you can kiss a girl."

Fire burned beneath her breastbone and crawled north up her neck, igniting her cheeks. She kept her eyes firmly focused on the screen even though she couldn't recite what happened even if she were offered fifty million dollars. "So you think you know how to kiss better?"

He lifted one shoulder and set his drink on the stand beside the sofa. "I know a few things. Like he doesn't tilt his head enough. And he should touch her. Her hand or her arm or her waist." He gave her a smirk and winked. "That's something Wyatt taught me."

She lifted her leg onto the couch and angled it beneath her as she turned to face him. "So teach me."

Almost as soon as the words left her lips, she wanted to suck them back in. This was a bad idea. A friendship ending level bad idea.

Or maybe not. It was just Dean, after all. Surely a small kiss couldn't have the power to change their weird little bond that had been solid for seven years.

Dean's sapphire eyes widened. "Y-you mean you want to kiss me?"

An immediate "yes" danced on the tip of her tongue and nearly made it free. "No, of course not, but if you're so experienced and you can spot all the things he's doing wrong, maybe you could teach me how to do it right before my next date."

A dark cloud passed over his face and he quirked a single brow. "And exactly when is that and with who?"

Jillian heaved a sigh. "It's hypothetical, Sparky. I just want to be prepared." She frowned and lifted one shoulder. "Hey, if you aren't as great as you say, you

135

can feel free to back out now."

Dean scooted forward until his knee bumped hers. "Is that a challenge, Jillybean?"

She smirked. "You're the one bragging about your talents."

His eyes darted from her face to the TV to the archway that led from the hall into the room and back to her again. "You're not gonna…get all girly on me after this, are you?"

Jillian drew her brow together. "'Get all girly?'"

"Yeah." He reached up and rubbed the back of his neck. "You know, start acting like you wanna be my girlfriend or something like that."

She snorted and moved slightly closer to him, her leg wedging beneath his. "Listen, Sparky, you're cool and you're fun and you're the best friend I've ever had, but that is definitely not going to happen."

"Okay."

With that single word he leaned forward and moved a hand to grip the back of her neck. A swarm of butterflies beat their wings against her stomach as he inched nearer. When his mouth was a breath away from hers, he paused and she would have been certain her heart stopped beating as well if it weren't for the loud thumping in her ears.

His lips brushed softly on hers once, then twice before his mouth clung to hers with soft, gentle motions that would have tickled if she hadn't been lost in a moment and in a…feeling?

She moved to hold onto his shoulders and he adjusted the angle of his head, deepening the kiss slightly and tracing her lower lip with his tongue. When she looked back on that slice of their relationship, she could never pinpoint exactly how long it lasted, but the loud opening and closing of the kitchen door heralding his parents' return ended it earlier than it would have on its own.

Despite the churning in her gut, the blood raging inside her like whitewater rapids, and the lack of oxygen in her lungs, she affected a nonchalant smile and silently hoped her best friend couldn't see through it. Or at least wouldn't call her out on it.

"Not too bad, Sparky. Maybe you have a future as a consultant for the next round of eligible men seeking true love among thirty women in nine weeks."

He snorted and grinned. "I'm gonna go see if Mom and Dad need help carrying stuff in."

Just as he rounded the back of the couch she turned on her knees and leaned over it. "Oh, see if they have ice cream!"

Chapter Fifteen

Dean

Present Day

For the fifth time Dean flipped over on the couch, trying desperately to find a position comfortable enough to finally fall asleep while knowing his insomnia had nothing to do with the sofa and everything to do with the memory of Jillian's lips on his. The reality of kissing an all-grown-up Jillian had nothing on their past teenage experiments or the fantasies he'd concocted in his own head.

Just as the first fingers of light began to stretch across the sky, Dean's eyes finally closed and stayed that way until the strong aroma of fresh coffee teased his nose and pried his lids apart. He rolled onto his side and propped himself up on one elbow to look over the back of the couch and into the kitchen where Jillian was moving around.

She turned from the refrigerator to the island and jumped slightly when her gaze landed on him. "You're awake."

Dean groaned, fell back onto the pillow, and threw an arm over his eyes. "That's the rumor." After a few moments he summoned the energy to sit up and plant his feet on the floor. "I've never needed coffee more in my life."

He padded into the kitchen, attempting to step around Jillian as she assembled two breakfast sandwiches and heaped fried potatoes onto plates. Just as he filled his cup and moved to grab creamer from the fridge, she turned and they bumped into each other.

Simultaneous "I'm sorry's" jumbled together and ended with Jillian heaving a hefty sigh. Her emerald green eyes locked onto his and his stomach churned.

She set the dishes on the table and leaned her hip against the surface. "Time to talk, Sparky." She pulled her chair out, sat down, and gestured to his normal place at the table.

Dean fixed his coffee and took a seat diagonal to the one Jillian occupied. "Whatcha need to talk about?" As if he didn't know. As if he hadn't spent his entire night reliving every caress of her lips on his. As if he didn't want to take this chance to tell her how he really felt for her.

"We've both been weird around each other since last night and that's the last thing I want to happen to our friendship, much less to have that hanging over us for this..." she gestured between the two of them "...thing."

His lips twitched with a repressed grin. "You mean marriage. The word is marriage. Wedded bliss. Happily ever after. Riding off into the sunset—"

She held up one hand. "All right, Sparky, let's not

get carried away. You know what I mean." She dropped the fork she'd been holding and laid her hand on top of his, squeezing slightly. "There is nothing in this world worth ruining our friendship. You've been the only constant in my life since I was seven years old. I...don't want to lose that."

Dean shoved a small mountain of ketchup-covered fried potatoes into his mouth, not pulling away from the light grip she held on his other hand. The tangy taste didn't even register as he focused on her words and weighed the wisdom of saying the "L" word that danced on the tip of his tongue nearly every time he was in her presence.

"That's never going to happen." The conviction he added to the assertion belied his true feelings. The fear that going too far too fast would end with his heart not only broken because she didn't love him, but because he'd lose his best friend.

"You are more important to me than any issue my family has. If we need to call off this fake marriage thing because it's causing problems between us, I'll do that in a heartbeat."

His own traitorous heart cracked slightly. "You think last night was a problem?"

Crimson stained her cheeks and she ducked her head. "Not...necessarily. But I don't want things to get confusing or for you to get hurt. We're doing a lot of pretending in front of people." She drew in a deep breath. "And outright lying. I-I just don't want things getting too complicated."

He turned his hand beneath hers and laced their fingers together. "It wasn't the first time we've ever kissed and we survived that just fine."

A small smile curled her lips and she looked up at him from beneath her lashes. "That was different. We were kids and we were just...experimenting."

Looking back, Dean was almost certain he was beginning to fall in love with her then, but was just too stupid to realize it. "And this time we are practicing for our wedding day to make it very convincing." He gave her a wink that was far more confident than he truly felt. Which was incredibly annoying since this girl was the only one who managed to make him unsure about anything.

She pressed her lips together and pinned him with a suspicious stare. "So we're okay?"

"We're okay. It was a moment that was bound to happen." He narrowed his gaze and affected the most disapproving scowl he could muster. "That doesn't mean you can get shit-faced and make stupid decisions tonight."

Jillian propped her elbows on the table and buried her face in her hands with a groan. "Oh hell, I forgot that was tonight." She kicked him lightly beneath the table as she resumed eating her breakfast. "No hooking up with a random stripper, either."

Dean snorted and took a huge bite of his sandwich. "You realize that my bachelor party is being organized by my three very married, very in love, and mostly very boring brothers." He swallowed. "And Mat, but he doesn't count because he's still getting over the whole divorce thing."

The phone still lying on the end table in the living room chirped to life. Dean frowned as he stood to retrieve it, wondering who the hell would be texting him this early on a Saturday morning.

As soon as he swiped across the screen a smile curled his lips. Between the kiss that rocked his world and the sleepless night that followed, he'd almost forgotten about the surprise he'd somehow managed to pull off just in time for Jillian's night out with the girls.

"Hey, I'm gonna hop in the shower. I've got a few things to do before tonight." He tilted his head. "We're okay, right?"

Jillian turned her lips inward as she stood and crossed the room. She wrapped her arms around his waist and hugged him tight. "As long as you're my best friend, we're okay."

The woman was tearing him apart from the inside out and didn't have a clue. He held her close, both reveling in and cursing the moment. And hoping against hope that somehow he could make her fall in love with him.

Letting her go might kill him.

***

Jillian

Present Day

After she secured the twentieth bobby pin in place, she turned slightly in the mirror and nodded, happy to have her ginger locks high on her head with a few rings cascading down each side. For the third time she quickly crossed to the window when she heard a loud engine, hoping Dean would be home.

Sooner than she wanted, she'd be faced with the bridal party of her mother's dreams and she'd spend the night pretending to have fun with whatever they had planned. Her saving grace was that Dean's sisters-in-law had agreed to come along as well.

All except a very pregnant Georgia who Jillian promised a special night out with after she delivered her and Wyatt's second child.

Jillian groaned as she applied a swipe of pink lip gloss across her lower lip and pressed them together. Next to Dean, Angela was her closest friend and her heart ached to have her miss this event.

Even if it was a party to celebrate the biggest lie of her life.

"Honey, I'm home," Dean called out from the front of the house, silencing the avalanche of thoughts causing her temples to throb.

She smoothed a hand over the front of her asymmetric ivory dress before exiting the bedroom and promptly stopped still at the periphery of the living room, her bare toes touching the edge of the area rug covering the hardwood floor. Her gaze narrowed in on his mischievous smirk. "What are you up to?"

His eyes widened and he clasped an excessively dramatic hand to his chest. "Why, Jillybean, how could you ever think I'd hold something back from my betrothed? What an awful implication."

Jillian arched a single brow and ignored the pinprick at her conscience at his comment. "It certainly wouldn't be because you're guarding the door like a dopey pit bull, now would it?"

He folded his arms across the chest—the one that was so much broader and stronger than she remembered—and attempted to affect a stern glare. But the twitching of his lips gave him away. "Dopey pit

143

bull? With that attitude, I'd take your gift back if it were returnable, Ms. Monroe."

Her fingers toyed with the delicate embroidered flowers along the hem of the sheer overlay of her dress. "Gift?"

A wide smile took up residence on his face. "I know you haven't exactly been looking forward to any of this with your merry little band of Stepford wives in the making as your bridal party." His humorous stare turned soft. "And since I'm currently filling the role of dashing groom, it would be a little weird for me to be there for girl's night, so I got the next best thing."

Dean stepped to one side and pulled open the door. Her mouth fell open as her gaze landed on Angela standing on the other side of the threshold with a giant suitcase next to her feet.

"Surprise," the other woman exclaimed as she threw her arms open wide and ran over to her, pulling her into a tight embrace. "Damn, I've missed you."

Tears burned at the corners of Jillian's eyes as she held Angela in a firm, long hug. "You have no idea," she agreed in a small voice.

Angela finally released her and stepped to the side, scanning up and down the length of Dean's body with open appreciation. "You failed to mention your best friend was a mega hottie."

A white flash of something she couldn't quite identify shot through her at Angela's off-handed comment. Something she hadn't experienced since she was a teen...and she'd been confronted with Dean's annoyingly large female fan club when she'd joined his parents in picking him up from school once. She grabbed Angela's hand and tugged her toward the

144

bedroom. "That's my fiancé to you, you shameless hussy." Her grin took the bite from the words. "Let's find you something to wear."

Jillian led Angela in the direction of the bedroom, but paused for half a second in the doorway before turning to sprint across the floor to launch herself in Dean's arms, barely giving him a chance to set down the luggage he'd just pulled through the door. "How can you possibly keep being so amazing when I'm being a complete pain in the ass?"

His grip tightened infinitesimally. "You're half a pain in my ass. Only my brothers have the honor of being complete pains in my ass."

Dean had always had a thoughtful streak, especially where she was concerned, but his selfless attentiveness lately was more than she'd ever seen from him. He had grown up while she'd been criss-crossing the globe and…

A small corner of her heart ached. He was both the same Dean who was her rock and biggest supporter and a whole new being she had an inexplicable draw to.

It was a pretty damn confusing complication that she really didn't need. The reincarnation of the teenage crush she thought she'd put to bed long ago was most definitely not what she needed right now.

And it was a thought that played on a loop through her brain the entire night. The mixture of inexplicable feelings and ideas swirling through her mind since their kiss became more muddled and cloudier with each gin and tonic set before her that rapidly found its way to her gut.

The dense fog of alcohol blanketed her as Angela bundled her into a car she didn't recognize and then led her up the few steps to Dean's front door. Angela cursed loudly when the knob didn't turn and then awkwardly knocked while Jillian struggled to keep her balance. She knew she was failing when Angela reached out for the railing, stumbling under Jillian's weight.

Dean yanked open the door wearing only pajama pants and an obnoxious grin. Obnoxious, adorable, whatever.

She pointed at him and fell against his bare chest. "There's my sexy fiancé." She turned back to Angela. "You can go to a hotel for the night...we need some alone time."

Dean scooped her up and held her close to him. "No, we don't, you can take the bed and I'll keep this one in the living room. It's closer to the bathroom for the inevitable porcelain worship that will be happening."

Angela patted his bicep as she moved past him. "Good luck, Romeo."

"Hey, keep your mitts off my...my..." She tilted her head and looked at him. "What are you again?"

He chuckled and gently laid her on the couch. "I'm the guy who is going to be holding your hair back while you empty the contents of your stomach into my toilet."

Before he could straighten his back, she reached up to grab his face. "You're the guy who is saving my entire family because my father kept betting it all on lady luck showing up in the next hand."

Dean sat on the edge of the cushion beside her. "What do you mean?"

The warm fingers of oblivious sleep tugged on her conscious and her lids drooped in response. "That's why I need this. Need you." She snuggled deeper into the cushions of the sofa. "My dad gambled away everything, even put the glass castle on the line." She giggled. "You always came up with the best nicknames."

A long breath exited Dean's mouth. "That's why you need the money. It isn't for you, it's to save them."

She gave a single nod and let her eyes shut. "Yup."

In the distance she could hear the deep rumbling baritone of his voice, but none of his words made sense as she allowed herself to be drug into the dreamless slumber the excessive amount of alcohol she had consumed offered.

Chapter Sixteen

Dean

Eleven Years Ago

"Yeah, I'll pick you up at seven tonight." He paused and turned, biting back a groan when he spied Connor standing in his doorway. "Okay. Sounds good. Okay. Bye."

He clicked off the phone call and pinned his older brother with an annoyed stare. "Eavesdropping is rude, ya know."

"Are you and Jillian going on a date?" Connor asked in a sing-songy voice punctuated by kissy faces and smacking sounds.

Dean narrowed his eyes and straightened his spine to his full height...which still left him dwarfed by his older brother by several inches. "First of all, she's my best friend, not my girlfriend. Guys and girls are capable of just being friends, ya know. The three of you are a bunch of assholes for saying otherwise. And second, I'm going out with Jenny Taylor's younger sister." He smirked at his older brother. "You remember Jennygs, right? The girl who shot you down?"

Connor rolled his eyes and huffed away, but not before Dean caught the stain of crimson on his cheeks.

His phone chirped to attention and he looked down to see Jillian's name flash across his screen. How could his brothers possibly think he liked her? It was *Jilly*. "Hey, Jillybean, what's up?"

"Hey, Sparky, listen up. They just released the last season of our show to stream. I'll talk Frieda into making Black Forest cake…"

In spite of all his assertions to Connor, he had a small moment of hesitation before telling Jillian he had plans with another girl…even though he wasn't entirely certain why. "Sorry, Jilly, I can't tonight. I have a date."

He winced as he added the final part, not sure why he felt the need to say it and not sure why it was a big deal.

This is just Jilly. She's barely even a real girl. It was a mantra he'd repeatedly said to his brothers, but never before really had to tell himself.

She quickly switched gears and everything between them went back into normal territory. "Oh, who is it? I need information here, Sparky. Name, rank, social security number. First date? Second date? And where are you taking her? Your unromantic ass better pick somewhere decent."

Just like that they slid back into their normal back and forth banter, he threw thinly veiled insults at her mother and she desperately tried to attack his healthier than normal ego.

"Hey, I expect a call to let me know how this goes. I'm placing bets on this being another who can't

149

manage to deal with you." Her giggle shone through the cough she tried to cover it with. "I barely make it through some days."

He huffed, only barely keeping his own laughter in check. "All right, all right. I get it. It's national give Dean shit day."

"If I didn't, you'd think you had some sort of terminal disease that was making me be all nice and sweet to you. Besides, if you play your cards right, I'm sure your hot date tonight would be more than happy to kiss your emotional boo-boos and make them all better."

After a few more good natured back and forth jabs, he disconnected the call and prepared for his date, ignoring the still uneasy feeling in his gut and the tendrils of Jillian that wrapped around his mind and refused to let go.

He was on the final button of his robin egg blue shirt when he realized that it had been a gift from Jillian and he had a brief erratic thought that maybe his subconscious was trying to tell him something. But he just as quickly dismissed the idea for the pure bullshit it was.

Although maybe it wasn't total bullshit if he found himself comparing Alana to Jillian. Each time he'd wrangle his disobedient mind into control and focus on his date, but sooner rather than later, he'd find himself thinking about his best friend once more.

Jillian would never talk through a movie.

And she wouldn't force him to share food over dinner.

And she most definitely wouldn't hang on his arm and feign fear during a decidedly unscary part of the movie. Hell, it was an action film. Who in their right mind would find that scary?

Nope, Jillian would be punching his arm and telling him he'd be far too big a weenie to tackle the stunts being played out on the big screen. And most likely drop an ice cube down the back of his shirt.

As he dropped Alana off at home and drove home he decided he would definitely need to go back to see it again with Jillian. And possibly scratch movies off the list for dates unless he found a girl as cool as her to go with.

***

Jillian

Eleven Years Earlier

Jillian tossed a piece of popcorn at Dean with a grin. "How was your love connection?"

He shrugged and took a long drink from his water, beads from the glass falling on his shirt. "We're going out again next week."

An unexpected blow connected with her abdomen at his words. Dean had dated before, way more than her, but this time it all hit her differently. She worked to keep her tone even, and even happy, while on the phone with him, but she'd been in a foul mood all evening.

Hearing that this was all happening again wasn't what she'd expected...and for some strange reason it really wasn't something she was thrilled about. "So you had fun?"

"I don't know about fun." He looked over at her with

a smirk just as a petty, verbal sparring match broke out on the screen in front of them with three female contestants trading barbs and slurs, all in the name of fake love. "Girls are weird."

She shoved an elbow into his ribcage. "Hey, rude. I'm a girl, you know."

He nudged her with his shoulder. "Barely. You're my Jillybean. You know you're different."

An odd grip of unease clamped down on her stomach. Her mouth dried and her tongue clung to the roof of her mouth. She didn't really know what she expected from him, but it certainly wasn't that. And it most definitely wasn't hearing that she was "just Jillian."

She turned down her lips and drew her brows together. "What exactly does that mean?"

Dean lifted one shoulder again and she barely resisted the urge to smack him for his completely nonchalant attitude. Not to mention his total ignorance of her intentionally hard to miss warning tone. "You're my best friend. We have fun when we're doing literally nothing. You aren't looking to be wined and dined and impressed. I can relax and just be with you."

Her eyes shouldn't have filled with tears at his words.

And she shouldn't have a lump in her throat.

And she most definitely should not look at that statement as being one of the biggest compliments of her life.

But they did and she did and it was. No matter what stupid notions popped into her head where Dean was concerned, at the end of the day they'd be friends and it would be easy and they'd have each other.

She swallowed down the flame of jealousy that had flared when he'd first announced his date that fanned into a larger blaze with the knowledge that this was more than a one time thing. It was an unusual feeling and one she wasn't really happy with. This was Dean and they were friends. She'd never wanted anything different…until she sort of did.

She took a large drink of water and focused her attention back on the TV screen. It was a ridiculous and potentially dangerous idea.

Teenage boys weren't exactly known for their maturity and Dean more than fulfilled the childish role. The youngest in the family had been just slightly indulged more than the others and his attitude sometimes showed it. If she let on, even just a little, that she was starting to see him in a different light with each inch he grew taller and the progressive deepening of his voice that somehow began popping up in her dreams, he'd probably get hives at the very thought.

Her head was swimming in conflicting and confusing ideas and his bark of laughter from beside her jolted her back to reality. "What the hell are you laughing at?"

Dean laid a hand to his stomach with a light smack. "I-I-I can't even…I have to rewind this." He grabbed the remote and clicked the DVR backward a few scenes. "Check this out. Big bro man here gets completely trashed and winds up…you've just gotta see it."

Jillian's amusement at drunken stupidity transformed into horror as the young man's drunken antics resulted in a complete loss of control of nearly every bodily function at the same time. And on national television.

She reached over and grabbed his arm. "Promise me you'll never let me make that big of a fool of myself, drunk or otherwise."

"Scout's honor." He held up three fingers on his right hand, his thumb and pinky touching near his palm.

She pressed her lips together in a thin line. "You were never a boy scout. Totally meaningless."

He grinned. "You know I'll never let anything happen to you, drunk or sober."

Jillian settled deeper into the couch and laid her head on his shoulder, keeping a firm grip on his forearm. "I know, Sparky."

Chapter Seventeen

Dean

Present Day

He glanced over at Jillian's still slumbering form before adding the final scoop of grounds to the basket, closing the lid, and pressing the button to start the coffee he knew she'd be desperate for as soon as she woke. The single serve dispenser he normally used wasn't going to be enough to tackle the drum line he was certain she'd have playing in her head.

Dean rested his backside against the counter and took a long drink from the glass of orange juice he'd abandoned long enough to start the coffee. Jillian's drunken declaration from the night before played through his head once again.

My dad gambled away everything.

A twinge of pain had been his immediate reaction. Why did it take excessive amounts of alcohol to elicit the final piece of the puzzle?

Even as the question formed in his mind, he

155

answered it on his own. For better or worse, no matter how much she bucked every tradition and proprietary behavior her mother tried to force down her throat, Jillian loved her family and was devoted to them. Addiction was a painful pill for loved ones to swallow no matter what form it came in.

And certainly Brad*ford*—even in his head, he'd always added a little extra disgusted emphasis to the second half of her brother's name because he found it to be the most pretentious name ever—couldn't be bothered to help out in anyway. The tech company he ran from his seven bedroom villa in Phuket, Thailand was the only thing her brother cared about.

Dean gave a soft snort. As much as it annoyed him, he almost understood the eldest Monroe child's continental move. Helena was an oppressive beast.

A small smile teased the corners of his mouth. In spite of her mother's best efforts to mold Jillian into a cookie cutter version of herself, the feisty redhead had lived up to every personality trait attached to her ginger hair. She knew what she wanted for her life and lived it out exactly as she'd envisioned, no matter the backlash she received.

"Oh shit, oh shit, oh shit." The string of curses accompanied the banging of limbs against wood as Jillian scrambled to rise from the couch, find her footing, and sprint to the bathroom.

Dean chuckled to himself as he trailed behind her, fully prepared to hold her hair or wipe her face with a wet washcloth. He sat on the side of the tub next to the toilet and gently stroked his fingers up and down her spine when the vomiting dissolved into sobs.

She slid on her knees closer to him, laying her head

in his lap. "Why the hell did you let me go out last night?"

He shook his head. "I like how you managed to make this my fault." He reached over to the faucet in the tub and soaked the cloth he'd barely been able to grab with his fingertips.

Jillian shivered slightly as he pressed the cold material to the back of her neck then melted into him with a marginally contented sigh. "That's what white knights do, Sparky. If you're gonna play the role, you gotta fulfill every part."

"Who was the culprit last night?" He stroked her back gently, not missing any opportunity to touch her and kept his voice at a low tone to avoid sending a spike through her undoubtedly aching brain.

"My nemesis." She mumbled into the denim covering his leg. "Tequila. It started out all innocent like with a margarita or two. Then Ainsley decided we needed to do shots."

Imagining the perfectly styled and utterly proper girls her mother had roped into being her attendants getting shit-faced on tequila shots elicited a bark of laughter from Dean that had Jillian gripping her skull and groaning. He winced slightly. "Sorry, Jillybean."

They sat in silence for a few more minutes before he bent at the waist to bring his lips close to her ear. "Want some help back out to the couch?"

She nodded her head without moving it from his lap which, unfortunately for Dean, meant that it caressed his thigh in a way that tested his limits of self-control. Only the internal reminder that he didn't want to irreparably screw this up and certainly didn't want to take advantage of Jillian hung over kept his jeans from

157

getting tight.

Well, too tight anyway.

With one arm around her waist, he guided her back to the sofa and tucked the thick blanket around her securely. "Coffee now or later?"

Red rimmed eyes peeked out from over the edge of the comforter she'd pulled up to nearly cover her face. "I'm sorry I didn't tell you sooner."

Without a single cell in his brain participating in the action, he leaned forward and kissed her forehead softly. "I get it. It's hard to talk about."

She scooted deeper into the cushions and looked up at him with a slightly lost and completely pathetic expression that sent an arrow straight into his hopelessly in love heart. "Lay with me? Just for a little while?"

Before she'd even finished speaking, he was stretching out on the couch beside her. Like there was a chance in hell he'd be anywhere else.

***

Jillian

Present Day

Someone glued sandpaper to the inside of her eyelids.

That was the first thought that popped into Jillian's head when she tried to open her eyes, followed quickly by the realization that for the first time in nearly a decade she had to have eaten meat. Raw, rancid meat. That was the only explanation for the horrific taste clinging to her tongue.

She scrambled over the top of Dean's slumbering form to race to the bathroom and scrub away the evidence that she'd had way too much to drink and had subsequently emptied the contents of her stomach when she woke earlier. She groaned as she assaulted her teeth with the brush liberally coated with paste as the memories of the previous night as well as her undoubtedly charming earlier worship at the altar of the porcelain god replayed in her head.

After two rounds of mouthwash and a quick splash of cold water over her face, she finally emerged from the bathroom. With a quick glance to confirm Angela was still sleeping on the other side of Dean's closed bedroom door, she padded back into the living room. The enticing aroma of coffee tugged her slightly to the right where Dean was filling an enormous white mug at the kitchen counter.

"Black and strong," he softly announced as he handed her the warm cup. "Luckily, your nap was short enough that the auto off didn't kick in, so it's still nice and hot."

She took a small sip of the steaming brew and looked up at him. "You deserved better than that." He opened his mouth but she held up her hand to silence him. "I know you're going to argue to try to make me feel better, but I was an ass. I should have laid it all out to you from the beginning."

At least half a dozen expressions cycled across his face, but she couldn't identify a single one until his mouth settled into a cocky grin that didn't quite reach his eyes. "I shouldn't enjoy you admitting you're an ass this much, should I?"

Jillian shot him a narrowed glare and thumped his chest with the back of her hand. "You're not making this easy, Sparky."

"That was never part of this bargain." He chuckled lightly and took a step closer to her. "But I accept your apology, soon-to-be Mrs. Carlisle."

She twisted her lips to the side and squinted. "Mrs. Monroe-Carlisle." It was important to her not to lose the strong tie to her grandfather, even for the brief period of time their union would last. Although she knew Dean wasn't the traditional type, she'd hesitated mentioning her plan to keep her last name. Another less than stellar decision.

"That has a mighty fine ring to it." Dean tapped his own coffee mug lightly against hers. "Happy Day Before Marriage, Mrs. Monroe-Carlisle."

There wasn't a single second of their interaction that was sexy or enticing. Not a moment that would incite romance or desire.

Yet as she stood in the small kitchen of his townhome with him, a powerful wave of lusty need swept over her and Jillian began plotting against her best friend...in the best way possible.

Certainly their two-decade-old relationship would be strong enough to survive adding sex to their fake marriage bargain. And it was most definitely a benefit Dean deserved for giving up his freedom for her.

Chapter Eighteen

Dean

Ten Years Earlier

"I don't think that's a good idea." Dean slung the beach towel around his neck and shifted on his feet. A slither of discomfort snaked its way down his spine. When had discussing girlfriends and dating with Jillian become so uncomfortable? Hell, when had anything become uncomfortable with Jillian?

She was the one person, even more so than his brothers, that he could relax with. Hanging out with Jillian was probably the calmest he ever was.

Even though he did his best to come off almost as cocky as Wyatt and nearly as confident as Tanner, he couldn't help but wrestle with an invisible weight of expectation. One that had never really been spoken, but one that lay heavily on his shoulders.

Tanner had practically been born in a three-piece suit and seamlessly stepped into his role at Carlisle International straight out of college.

For as long as Dean could remember, Wyatt ate, drank, and breathed the rodeo...to the extent that his parents had built a barn and stocked it with two horses and damn near every riding accessory needed to help Wyatt train to realize his dream.

And Connor was the epitome of ridiculous. An annoying combination of artistic talent and brains meant his brother could do damn near anything. It was only made worse by the fact that Connor was the most sensitive of all the boys and Dean's ally against the two oldest who made torturing Connor and Dean their life's mission sometimes.

But Dean...he didn't really know his purpose. Most of the time he didn't care, but he had an occasional twinge of jealousy at all three of his brothers' focused paths in life. None of them wavered or doubted, just pursued the goals they'd long ago made.

He'd entertained everything from becoming a lawyer to an accountant to a veterinarian and practically everything in between. Nothing felt right, but nothing really felt wrong either. He could probably live with nearly any job, but he didn't feel the pull or passion that he saw in his siblings.

But none of that mattered when he was with Jillian. He could kick back and just be Dean and that was enough for her.

Until now.

Which was annoying as hell.

She planted her fists on her hips and gave him an irritated glare. "Exactly what's wrong with a double date?" She lightly punched his bicep. "Ashamed to introduce your girlfriend to your best friend?"

He rolled his eyes and climbed in the bed of Wyatt's

162

old truck that his brother had left behind when he moved out of town in search of the rodeo fame he'd always dreamt of. He laid the towel on the bed liner and stretched himself out, the early September sun beating down on him, drying his damp skin. "You ought to know that girls get weird about stuff like that."

Jillian flicked the edge of the terrycloth she'd hastily wiped over her freckled shoulders spreading it out beside him. "That's just dumb." She rotated her head and lifted her sunglasses. Before he even met her penetrating stare, he knew she was definitely ready to lay down the law according to Jillian. "If she doesn't like me then clearly she isn't good enough for you."

He smirked at her, squinting against the bright sunlight. "Got your bossy pants on there, Jillybean?"

She grinned in response and slid her sunglasses back in place. "Never leave home without them, Sparky."

Dean shifted slightly on the towel. "Fine, fine, we'll do this double date crap."

"Good." She lifted her head far enough to hold her mass of hair on top of her head before laying back down and letting the wet tendrils fan out around her. "I'll take care of all the arrangements."

He groaned. "Sounding like the Ice Queen there, Jillybean. We don't need to be going all fancy here. My pinky doesn't stick up when I drink. Biologically impossible." A smile tugged at his lips. "Ya know, being 'new money' and all."

His comment was rewarded with a sharp elbow to his ribs and then a second jab when he chuckled in response to the first.

"Dinner and movies casual enough for you, Casanova-wannabe?"

A wave of gratitude washed over him that the fleeting moment of discomfort had passed and they had easily fallen back into just being them. "That works for me. Just make sure your little preppy boyfriend knows how to wear something other than button down shirts and sweater vests."

"Sure thing, Sparky, as long as you tell your girlfriend to ditch the halter tops and Daisy Dukes."

Her quick retort brought out an immediate bark of laughter.

He held up three fingers, his thumb and pinkie touching near his palm. "I will make sure she is on her best behavior. Scout's honor."

Jillian yawned. "You were never a scout so that isn't exactly comforting."

He turned his head to face her and stared at her just slightly longer than normal. Had her nose always turned up slightly at the tip and looked that cute? He blinked a few times. What the hell was that kind of thought? This was Jillian. "When do you want to commence with the torture…I mean plan this double date?"

"Maybe in a few weeks? I have a heavy course load right now and need to get a little more grounded in it before I get all distracted by Spencer in a sweater vest."

Dean groaned at her giggle and laced his fingers behind his head, letting the heat from the sun and the exhaustion from a day swimming in the lake pull him into a light sleep.

***

Jillian

Ten Years Ago

Dean pulled off the end of the covering of his straw and blew into the tube, shooting the paper at Jillian across the table. She balled up the wrapper and tossed it back at him with a smirk.

Spencer huffed in the booth beside her and warmth crept up the back of her neck when she realized she'd very nearly forgotten her very new boyfriend was sitting beside her.

She turned slightly in her seat and focused on Spencer. "What did you think of the movie?"

Small crinkles formed around his chocolate eyes as he slid his arm along the back of the bench seat and his thumb stroked her shoulder. "It was a bit predictable and the humor was...rather immature."

Dean snorted across the table and tossed an entire jalapeno popper in his mouth. "Immature? You're almost seventeen, not forty. I think you just need to lighten up, my man."

Erica slid her hand inside the crook of Dean's left arm and scooted closer to him. "I thought it was funny. Although some of the fight scenes were just..." She shivered dramatically and Jillian fought the urge to roll her eyes.

Jillian shrugged in response. "They were okay. Not nearly as good as our favorite series, right, Sparky?"

He took a long drink from his soda then nodded vigorously. "I mean, I guess they did the best they could with no superheroes or otherworldly powers available to them."

The two easily fell into their normal post-movie discussion from the plot to the acting to hypothesizing whether or not a sequel would happen and, if so, what it could entail. The waitress came and dropped off their food and they only stopped talking to inhale large bites of their food.

On one of the few breaks, Erica folded her arms across her chest. "Dean, I'd like to speak with you outside, please."

Dean slid out of the booth and stood to the side, offering a hand to Erica as she moved across the seat and got to her feet beside him. He fell in step behind her, casting a glance over his shoulder to where Jillian and Spencer still sat, lifting his shoulders slightly.

Spencer let out a low whistle. "Can't say I blame her."

She speared her fork through lettuce, tomato, and cucumber, stuffing the mass of vegetables in her mouth. The familiar rebellious thrill shot through her knowing her mother would have a fit seeing her well-trained daughter eating a decidedly *not* petite bite of food. "What are you talking about?"

He lifted both brows, cutting through his chicken with a delicate finesse Jillian was certain her mother would have swooned over. "You two. You're behaving as though you and Dean are on a date and we are just accessories."

The half of the salad already in her stomach turned and the accuracy of his words burned her cheeks. They hadn't meant it, hadn't wanted to hurt Spencer or Erica, but she and Dean had been friends for nearly a decade. Turning off everything that was ingrained by this stage was practically impossible.

Spencer pulled the napkin from his lap, blotted invisible food residue from his lips, and folded the napkin on his empty plate, fork and knife lying side by side on top to signal he was finished just as they'd both been trained in cotillion class. An unnecessary gesture considering the casual atmosphere of the steak house, but one she knew he couldn't turn off if he tried.

"Listen, Jillian, I like you, but not enough to fight some dude."

Jillian choked on her mouthful of water and coughed as she set the glass down. "What the hell makes you think you have to fight Dean? That's absolutely insane."

Before he could answer, she caught Dean across the room, face flushed and mouth drawn into a tight line.

Spencer sighed and stood. "That's exactly what I mean. I'm sure your *friend* will take you home. Goodnight, Jillian."

Dean stared quizzically at her as Spencer pushed past him to leave the restaurant. How in the world had this night gone this wrong?

Chapter Nineteen

Dean

Present Day

Having his three older brothers with him in the room at the back of the country club made the space go from small to damn near claustrophobic. The necktie, which suddenly seemed far too tight around his throat, certainly wasn't helping the situation.

He'd barely managed to get it on because his hands were shaking so much. Tanner's penetrating stare only managed to contract the iron grip of nerves holding onto his stomach. Dean swallowed several times then tried to smile as effortlessly as possible. "What's that look for?"

A small half smile transformed Tanner's serious face. "For as much shit as we've given you over the years, I never actually thought the day would come when you and Jillian actually got married." He clapped the younger man on the back. "Hell, I didn't really think you'd ever make a commitment."

Everyone other than Wyatt believed the fictitious

168

moment to be real and Wyatt not only knew the truth of the arranged marriage, but Dean's feelings for Jillian as well. That meant that Dean could speak all the things he'd hidden from Jillian.

All the things he knew damn well he should have said before today arrived, but with each perfectly good opportunity he'd managed to chicken out.

"It's Jilly." He spoke her name with a reverence he hadn't before thought himself capable of, but like everything else, she changed it all. "I'm pretty sure I've actually been in love with her since I was seven years old, I was just too stupid to recognize it."

Wyatt settled deeper into one of the few chairs lining the room, kicked his booted feet up on another seat and crossed his ankles, pulling his ever present cowboy hat down over his eyes and leaning his head back. "So you're an idiot, this isn't news."

Shit. His brother was coming dangerously close to...

Why the hell had he trusted Wyatt?

Instead of actually saying that, he arched a brow and pointed at his brother, even though Wyatt couldn't see the action. "Me? You bailed on Georgia and barely pulled your head out of your ass far enough to win her back." He turned an accusatory finger to Tanner. "You nearly lost a frickin' Norman Rockwell idyllic life." He moved on to Connor. "And I don't really think you actually did anything wrong with Kelsey, but you get lumped in with those two assholes because you're here and share DNA."

Wyatt straightened in his chair, righting his hat enough to shoot Dean a dark glare. One mirrored by Tanner. Connor smacked the heel of his hand to his forehead.

169

"Nice inspirational speech, little brother."

Dean sighed and folded his arms in front of his chest. "All I'm saying is that we've all screwed up. Hell, Dad even screwed up once upon a time." Jillian flashed in front of his mind's eye. "And I wasted a lot of years, but I've gotten a second chance with her and I'm not going to lose the opportunity to prove how much I love her." His gaze swept over the three other men in the room. "I would think if anyone could understand that, it would be my brothers."

The tight lines at the corners of Tanner's eyes softened and a grin tugged at the corners of his mouth. "Basically all the Carlisle men are idiots who are lucky as hell we have very forgiving women."

Dean grinned. "Yeah, basically."

Tanner flicked his wrist then motioned toward Connor and Wyatt. "All right. Time for us to take our places."

As the other men got into position and waited for Jillian's attendants to arrive and take their arms, Dean took a moment in the silence of the small room and closed his eyes, breathing in deeply through his nose and slowly exhaling through his mouth. He was about to utter some very genuine vows to a girl who thought it was all a hoax to save her asshole of a father, her entire family.

Shit. He was just as big of an asshole for not opening his mouth and telling her sooner.

"Suck it up, buttercup," he whispered to himself as he finally left the room and took his place in line behind Connor just before his older brother stepped out onto the aisle. *You got yourself into one hell of a mess, now you just got to hope you can somehow find your way out of it without losing her.*

Dean took careful, measured steps down the white satin material the covered the ground between the two groups of seats. He plastered a smile on his face and did his damnedest not to wince when he saw the tears streaming down his mother's cheeks bracketing either side of her own broad grin.

He barely had a second to breathe when every atom of oxygen disappeared from his lungs. Jillian stood less than thirty feet from him in a gorgeous and—dammit all to hell—body hugging gown. Every delicate curve was accentuated in mouthwatering detail.

His knees nearly buckled beneath him as his gaze traveled up the front of the dress and his eyes feasted on the two small, pert orbs discreetly, but definitely noticeably showcased by the dip in the neckline.

Relief washed over him as she glided closer and he didn't see a trace of the concern or worry in her eyes he was so certain would greet him. Instead her emerald irises sparkled back at him and a smile that rivaled his own nearly blinded him.

Just as Jillian and her father stopped a foot in front of him, the magistrate that golfed at the club with her father said something just over Dean's right shoulder, but he couldn't recite a word of it if someone held a gun to his head. Mr. Monroe nodded and spoke and the next thing he knew the other man was giving her a hug, then sliding her hand into Dean's.

She lifted onto her tiptoes and put her lips close to his ear. "I know you're only doing this because you're frickin' amazing and you're bailing my ass out, but I wouldn't want to do something this stupid with anyone but you."

171

He grinned and winked as she pulled back and took her place by his side in front of the magistrate. "Right back atcha."

The truth niggled at the back of his mind, but Dean squashed the voice down into oblivion when the magistrate turned to him, waiting for him to recite his vows.

He took both of her hands in his and held firmly, a small measure of surprise crackling through him as she tightened their hold even more. "Jillybean, I love you." He poured every drop of sincerity he had into the handful of words, hoping she could somehow hear what he hadn't actually said. "You are my best friend. Today I give myself to you in marriage. I promise to encourage and inspire you, to laugh with you, and to comfort you in times of sorrow and struggle."

It was a vow that was a slight variation on the traditional, but neither of them were very traditional anyway. And it was absolutely perfect for the girl who had already been his best friend through three roller coasters' worth of ups and downs.

***

Jillian

Present Day

After the deep emotion that coated every word he spoke, she was fairly certain Dean should win an Oscar. And equally as sure that if she didn't rein in the troubling emotions that bubbled to the surface after a decade of being put to rest, she would wind up with a shattered heart in eighteen months when he earned his well-deserved freedom.

It was just the dress. It had to be. That and all the ridiculous emotions she'd been compartmentalizing ever since the first call from her mother. She couldn't really be entertaining the idea that she and Dean were actually getting married.

Oh shit. Shit, shit, shit, shit, shit. It was her turn. She straightened her shoulders slightly and nearly lost every conscious thought in Dean's sapphire gaze. Falling in love with the boy she'd shoved down romantic notions toward so long ago was absolutely, positively *not* part of the plan.

And yet it had somehow happened.

Fortunately for her, nearly everyone in the audience expected and wanted to see the level of love and commitment in both their vows that she accidentally somehow managed to feel for real.

"I love you, Dean. You are my best friend. Today I give myself to you in marriage. I promise to encourage and inspire you, to laugh with you, and to comfort you in times of sorrow and struggle."

If she didn't know better, she would swear there was a small drop collecting in the corner of his eye. But that was insane. Dean Carlisle hardly ever cried and certainly wouldn't be invested enough to do so now.

Unless he was mourning the loss of his bachelorhood and ability to have sex for the next eighteen months.

She dutifully held her hand out as Dean slipped the band on her finger, right beside the engagement ring she'd found herself staring at more and more.

"With this ring," he spoke the words so softly she could barely hear them, "I thee wed."

Ainsley, Jillian's maid of honor in name only, pushed Dean's wedding ring in her free hand. She swallowed against the tide of emotions clogging her throat. No. This could not be happening.

But as her eyes connected with his once more, her heart screamed out its truth.

Dammit all to hell, she'd fallen in love with her best friend. A-frickin-gain.

"With this ring, I thee wed." She wanted a damned glass of champagne. Not for celebrating their union, but as a reward for getting the words out without her voice cracking or the tears she was barely managing to contain spilling over onto her cheeks and streaking her mascara down her face.

Before the magistrate could even finish speaking, Dean snaked an arm around her waist and pulled her tight against him. He offered a wolfish grin half a second before he devoured her mouth. The soft gentle caresses that had started their unexpected kiss beneath the tree in the rainstorm a few days earlier was eclipsed by the brazen desire he poured out in this moment.

An Oscar, an Emmy, and a frickin' Tony. His acting was better than anything she'd seen on the big screen, the small screen, or Broadway.

Her responding enthusiasm, however, was wholly genuine. And fractured a small portion of her rapidly beating heart.

Long before she was actually ready, he broke the kiss and a mischievous smile curled his lips. "Piggyback ride?"

Her mouth fell open. "You mean here? Now?"

"Nothing would piss off the Ice Queen more and nothing else even comes close to being right for me and you."

She pulled on the delicate skirt of her dress until the hem hit just below her knee, giving her hips enough room. "I don't know when it happened, but somehow Dean Carlisle grew up to make very logical and rational arguments."

With that she hopped on his back, threw her arms around his neck, and completely ignored the bouquet Ainsley tried to give back. The majority of the guests erupted into cheers and laughter as they walked back down the aisle, but there was a near deadly silence from the area where her mother sat.

And she couldn't be happier about that fact.

He set her down just outside the doorway to the large room where they'd said their vows and she held his face with her hand to keep his gaze on hers. "Dean…"

Before she could find the words, the entire bridal party poured out of the room and surrounded them, Dean's brothers giving her kisses on the cheeks and telling her that welcoming her to the family was pointless since she'd been a member for two decades already.

They stood dutifully in the reception line, shaking hands, and giving hugs. Mike and Tracy Carlisle very nearly shattered her barely functional heart with the elation written all over their faces.

The evening continued the whirlwind pace, not allowing her the time to collect her scattered, confusing thoughts. They moved from table to table to speak with guests, but each time they approached a new one, the clanging of silverware against crystal wound up bringing their mouths together in almost constant kisses that left her even more perplexed than she had been seconds earlier.

When he collected her close to him for their dance, an idea popped into her head. She pressed even more firmly against him.

She could have blamed the champagne they'd drunk for the completely inappropriate path her brain was currently skipping down, but only two glasses after a heaping plateful of food and cake wasn't strong enough to be held responsible. Maybe tonight could be slightly more traditional than she once believed.

"You're my hero, you know that?"

He pulled back far enough to stare deep into her eyes without loosening his tight hold on her. "What?"

She sighed slightly and smiled. "You didn't have to do this. You didn't have to rescue me and you most definitely didn't have to help my family when they've been nothing but assholes to you. But you did. And you did it just because I asked...even before I drunkenly told you the whole story." She winced. "Sorry about that. Again."

His blue irises shimmered with amusement. "You're actually pretty damn cool when you're completely shit-faced." He brushed his lips across her cheek and moved to her ear. "And marrying you is my pleasure."

She turned her lips inward and bit down on them then laid her head on his chest.

The rest of the night she refused to release her hold on his hand. He gave her a single, quizzical look at first, then fell into the routine to keep up appearances.

Several hours later they arrived at the door of the luxury hotel suite Wyatt and Georgia had booked for them as a wedding gift after hearing they had no honeymoon plans. Dean swiped the keycard into the slot and propped the door open with one hip.

He laid a hand on her stomach, stopping her from entering. "What the heck, Jilly? Don't you know anything about weddings and thresholds and all that romantic shit?" His grin widened. "Are we gonna need to queue up the reality TV tonight to remind you?"

Words failed to leave her mouth as Dean put one arm behind her back and the other beneath her knees and lifted her close to his chest. Effortlessly he stepped across the threshold, punctuated by the door clicking closed behind them.

Their eyes locked in an intense stare she wasn't certain she could identify. Her heart screamed that she should confess her feelings, but the quiet voice of reason in her brain quickly brought her back to reality.

They might not have a happily ever after, but this next eighteen months certainly didn't need to a celibate bore. And she deserved a few happy memories to take with her when he left.

She set the small purse that matched her gown on the half-circle table placed by the entrance and turned to face him. "I have a proposition for you."

His mouth quirked into a half smile and he leaned back against the door. "I'm pretty sure you and your harebrained schemes are what got us hitched in the first place. What's your latest idea?"

Jillian closed the few feet between them. "Eighteen months is a hell of a long time for me to ask a Casanova like yourself to stay single."

His Adam's apple bobbed several times. "We talked about that. It's fine."

She shook her head slowly and tugged the tie free from around his neck. "You're my best friend and I trust you implicitly. Just because this isn't a normal, lovey dovey marriage doesn't mean it can't be…enjoyable."

His eyes widened to the size of saucers. The shock value would have been highly entertaining if every cell on her body wasn't buzzing with unfulfilled desire.

"Wh-what the hell are you getting at?"

"How would you feel about making this more like friends with some very fun benefits?" She took a deep breath, her bravado threatening to slip. "We care about each other, we trust each other, and, let's face it, you're pretty frickin' cute. What do you say?"

Chapter Twenty

Dean

Ten Years Earlier

Tracy Carlisle propped her hands on her hips and glared at her youngest son, a penetrating stare that never failed to make Dean squirm. "I don't think I remember making it an actual suggestion, I told you to do it."

But it's ridiculous, it's not like it's a date. He kept the comment and the attitude to himself, certain it would result in the loss of the car keys for a week at least. "Yes, ma'am, but it's just Jillian."

His mother lifted both her brows. "I don't care if you're taking one of Wyatt's horses as a date, when you take a girl to homecoming, you buy her a corsage. Now hurry up and see if you can find somewhere within a ten mile radius that hasn't already sold out."

Dean dropped his head and stared at his shuffling feet. "Yes, ma'am." He dutifully called local florists and cursed softly under his breath at the realization that his mother was right and he didn't find one that had

179

flowers in stock until the third one.

"What color is her dress?" He repeated the question to the woman on the other end of the call. "Well, how the heck am I supposed to know that?"

A damning sigh came across the line and made him frown into the phone as though the woman could see him. "Because she will want her corsage to match her dress. Could you imagine if you had a tiger lily corsage and a maroon gown? That would be an absolute atrocity."

Well, damn, this woman took her flowers pretty seriously. How the hell was he supposed to know this was such a big deal?

He scrubbed the back of his neck and cradled the receiver between his cheek and shoulder and slid his phone from his back pocket, his fingers flying across the screen as he sent Jillian a text he was certain she wouldn't answer in time. "Is there anything like...I don't know, generic?" He searched his brain and cursed the fact Connor wasn't around to give color advice. "Like wouldn't white work?"

Once again the clerk huffed and mumbled under her breath. Before she could admonish him again for some random floral faux pas he had no idea he was even committing, his phone sprang to life blaring out the pop tune he'd assigned to Jillian.

Saved by the obnoxious, overplayed song.

Jillian: It's dark blue. Although you asking, much less caring, is slightly concerning.

Dean typed back a "thanks" accompanied by the middle finger emoji. He cared about stuff. Maybe not dresses or flowers, but he cared about the shows she watched and what she wanted to do with her life. He cared about her dreams and her plans.

Wasn't that what really mattered? Not some stupid wrist bouquet. Who the hell came up with that thing anyway?

"Blue," he finally managed to blurt out the word. "Her dress is a dark blue. And she has red hair and green eyes." He had no idea why he felt the need to add that, but it was important.

For some really strange reason he didn't actually care about, that answer seemed to please the irritating woman on the other end of the phone. "Good, very good, I can work with that. It will be ready for pick up at five Saturday evening. We close at six, so please be prompt."

With that she hung up and he was left to stare at the phone. This was all getting way too weird. Since Erica broke up with him after the most ridiculous fight of his life, he just figured taking Jillian to the homecoming dance he'd already bought tickets for would be the easiest option.

That was a joke.

His mother leaned against the archway leading from the kitchen to the living room, her arms folded in front of her and a knowing smirk firmly in place. "Wasn't as easy as you thought, was it?"

Respect dictated he control his tone, but being the baby of the family did offer a few benefits. Mostly that, even though Connor liked to believe he was their mother's favorite child, she had a soft spot for her baby, the last child she would ever have.

So he knew he could offer an eye roll accompanied

181

by a slightly chagrined smile and not get reprimanded. "As usual, you were right. Which is kind of annoying."

Her grin widened in response. "There has to be some perks to being the mother of four boys."

Dean bent slightly at the waist and planted a kiss on his mother's cheek, a well-used tactic to stay firmly on her good side. "You mean other than having bragging rights for creating four spectacular specimens of mankind?"

She half snorted, half laughed and pushed off the wall, walking toward the backdoor and grabbing her garden gloves along the way. "Yeah, fantastic. When they aren't giving me headaches or heart attacks or backtalk."

***

Jillian

Ten Years Earlier

"But we have a gala scheduled tonight. You'll just have to cancel."

The utterly dismissive tone in her mother's voice set her teeth on edge. She couldn't count the number of events at her own school she'd missed because Helena required Jillian's presence at some ridiculous, over the top affair designed to make her mother look like the philanthropist of the year.

Jillian couldn't miss this. She'd not only promised Dean she'd go, she still held a measure of guilt over the fact that the only reason he even needed someone to go with him was because of the disastrous double date

182

she'd insisted on.

Her stomach churned at the memory of the night that ended with them both single. Yeah, she definitely needed to make this up to him.

"I'm sorry, Mother, but Dean has already purchased the tickets and I've picked out a gown." She schooled her face into as cold and aloof of a mask as she could. Basically just emulating her mother. "I won't be able to attend your gala function."

Helena's jaw worked back and forth in a barely perceptible motion, but one that Jillian was well attuned to. "I do not recall telling you that your presence was optional."

A small bead of fear iced Jillian's spine, but she straightened nonetheless, bringing herself to her full height. While Helena had never raised a hand to her, and never would, Jillian always had a need to please her mother in hopes of gaining some small amount of approval from the older woman. And to avoid the arctic silent treatment sure to follow any disappointing moments.

"I told you about this over a week ago, again last weekend, and three days ago." She pulled in a shaky breath, hoping her mother hadn't noticed the defect in her outward composure. "I have made a commitment, it would be unfair and irresponsible of me to break it. Besides, Bradford is home from VMI and you can," her tongue caught the word 'force' before it spilled free, "ask him to wear his uniform. I am sure that will be much more impressive than having me in attendance."

Unspoken was Jillian's full belief that her mother loved her brother more. That she could never quite measure up to the standard Bradford had set just by

183

being born a boy.

Rather than respond, Helena left Jillian to finish getting dressed in her room. The knot that had formed in her gut the moment her mother entered tightened a bit more. She was certain her mother would have some retribution for the entire event, most especially for Jillian's unwillingness to back down and give Helena what she wanted.

The brief discussion played on repeat in her head as she stepped into the blue gown, pulled it up onto her shoulders, and slid the zipper up the side. She eyed the ornate clock hanging on the opposite wall and quickly put her shoes on. She wanted to be downstairs and waiting before Dean showed up in case her mother felt the need to intercept.

Jillian would put absolutely nothing past Helena Monroe.

As she slipped her toe into her satin ballet slipper shoe a much more welcome voice greeted her ears. "Don't you look lovely tonight, darling."

The very first syllable pulled a wide smile from her and eased some of the Helena-induced tension in her stomach. She held out her hands to the older man approaching on her right. "Grandfather, you look dashing as always. New tux?"

He drew his bushy, gray brows together. "At my age? Bah! Why would I buy a new tux?" He lifted an arm and twirled her beneath it. "Unless my granddaughter requires someone a bit more dapper to dance with tonight."

She laughed lightly and rested a hand on his shoulder as she came to a stop. She desperately tried to ignore the fact that his cheeks were just slightly hollower than they had been before his latest trip to the hospital. "Sorry, Grandfather, I'm going to a dance with Dean tonight."

In an opposite reaction to what she'd expected, her grandfather's eyes brightened at her declaration and a spark of mischief twinkled at the corner. She'd long ago realized that one of the things she loved best about Dean was how close his personality was to her grandfather's.

Perhaps most girls gravitated toward men who reminded them of their father, but not Jillian. While her father was a mostly quiet and docile man, he was also rather absent, spending much of his time holed away in his library or at the club with friends. A fact her grandfather had noted and commented on more than once with choice words for his son.

"You are going to have a much better evening than I." He bent forward slightly and laid a soft kiss on her cheek. "And I do like that young man. Good to see he finally asked you out."

Heat crept up the back of her neck. "It isn't like that, Grandfather. We're just going as friends. His girlfriend broke up with him and he'd already bought tickets. It isn't a real date."

The older man cupped her jaw. "You never know when things may change."

Warmth spread up to her cheeks, engulfing her face in fire. He couldn't possibly know about that stupid crush she had on Dean…could he?

The doorbell rang, cutting through her muddled thoughts and her grandfather grinned. "That must be your young man."

Before Jillian could find the words to correct him, he

disappeared around the corner, undoubtedly heading toward the kitchen to pester Frieda and pilfer snacks before the gala commenced. Or possibly hunt down her father and give him another lecture on spending the evening holed up in his study playing poker or rummy or whatever he chose to overestimate his abilities on this time.

With a sigh she headed to the front door just as Henry pulled it open and stole every molecule of air from her lungs in the same moment. Dean stood on the other side of the threshold with a lopsided grin holding a delicate pink tissue paper-covered lump in one hand and sporting a perfectly tailored black suit that did absolutely nothing to help her dismiss the dozens of ideas about her best friend that had been playing on a loop since talking with her grandfather.

This was going to be a very, very long night.

Chapter Twenty-One

Dean

Present Day

"You're drunk."

He held his breath as he waited for her to respond and prayed to every god he could remember from his Greek mythology class that he wasn't dreaming.

Jillian smiled and his heart nearly quite beating. She popped the top button of his shirt free. And then the next one down. "Sparky, I had two glasses of champagne. You know me well enough to know it takes a hell of a lot more alcohol than that to get me drunk."

She pulled her lips between her teeth, intent eyes boring holes through the small, flimsy wall of chivalry he was desperately trying to cling to. Her finger circled the next button. "If you don't want me, if you don't want this…tell me to stop."

That word most certainly wasn't on his radar. But a mountain of concern and doubt was. "There isn't any sex in the world that is worth me losing you."

Her entire face softened. She moved her hand from his shirt to his jaw. "You are the only man in this world I know I can count on without even a shadow of a doubt. I have always known you'd be there for whatever I needed, but you proved even that to be an understatement when you agreed to basically sign away your life for damn near two years to just bail my sorry family out...just because I asked. There isn't anything in this universe or the next that could ruin that."

Now. Now was the time to tell her, to finally confess that he loved her.

She pressed her body to his and he gripped her hips, keeping her firmly in place. His tongue clung to the roof of his mouth as the heat from her flesh mixed with the smooth decadence of her satiny gown mixed in his grasp.

Damn it all to hell, maybe tomorrow he'd tell her. Because right now getting the woman of his dreams, the woman he loved, naked and writhing beneath him was not something he was willing to risk by opening his mouth.

Until he did.

"You don't owe me anything for that. I agreed to it because you needed help. I'm here because you're my best friend and I love you, and I wouldn't let you handle something that big on your own." He swallowed several times. "But you don't owe me anything, especially not this."

A salacious smile curled her lips and her fingers walked to the back of his neck, where she held on tight.

"What if I owe myself this? It's been a hell of a long time, Sparky." She rubbed herself lightly against him and he couldn't fight the shiver that trickled down from his head to his toes in response. "Besides, plenty of people have friends with benefits."

The words should have been an ice bucket to his libido and a samurai sword to his heart, but holding her this close was too much for him to resist. And the opportunity was too golden to allow it to slip through his grasp.

He groaned and dropped his mouth onto hers. It was damn near an instinct to allow himself to drown in her scent, her taste, her touch. He wasn't certain he'd survive the "benefits" she suggested once, let alone multiple times when simply kissing her practically drove him to his knees.

This woman was going to be the death of him.

She fisted his shirt and pulled him with her, their lips staying firmly locked as she walked backward toward the bed. When they both jolted from her legs reaching the bed, he slid his hands from her waist to cup her ass briefly before his fingers wandered up to the bottom button holding her dress on.

He tilted his head a little further and deepened the kiss as he slowly pushed each satin covered pearl through the hole. On the top one he paused and drug his mouth from hers. "We will still be best friends." It was a statement, a question, and his deepest fear all rolled into one.

Jillian nodded and swallowed, her chest heaving. "Always."

Dean groaned and freed the last button, letting the gown fall from her body. He sucked in a sharp breath at the curves on full display with a pathetic, but sexy as hell, excuse for lace underwear and a strapless bra barely covering her. "Dammit all to hell, Jillian, why didn't you tell me you had grown up?"

She tossed her head back and laughed, the waterfall of perfectly styled ginger curls falling over her shoulder. "You're the same age as me, Sparky. Didn't put two and two together until now?" She smiled. "Besides, you've seen me in a bikini more times than I can count." She stepped out of the circle of material pooled on the floor and reached behind her back.

His heart stopped as she flicked open the back of her bra and let it fall to the ground as well. She hooked her thumbs under the sides of her panties, shimmied her hips, and the slip of lace joined the rest of her clothes on the carpet.

This was it. This was absolutely how he was going to die. Just from looking at Jillian naked.

Not naked. His pants tightened to a level he wasn't certain was humanly possible. She was still wearing the five inch heels that had amazed him to watch her spin in with ease on the dance floor.

She bent over to pull one free and he set a hand on her shoulder, halting her movements. "Don't you dare."

Jillian straightened and smirked, arching a brow at him. She got on the bed and laid down, scooting toward the middle before she crossed her legs at the ankles. "Got some shoe kink going on there, Sparky?"

Within seconds he shed his jacket, shirt, and pants, whipping them across the room, unconcerned with where they landed until he only wore his boxer briefs. He stood at the foot of the bed and ran his fingers slowly up and down her calf. "Only on you."

He knelt on the bed and uncrossed her ankles, planting soft kisses from the top of her foot above the shoe to her hip bone and back down again on the other side. He moved up slightly and gripped her hips, his thumbs caressing the gently protruding bone.

"No matter what, you're my best friend."

She nodded and her voice came out far more strangled than it had been moments earlier. "No matter what, you're my best friend." The rebellious glint he'd come to expect from her sparkling gaze danced once more. "I'll even make sure to scream *Sparky* instead of baby or sweetie or honeybun."

He lowered his mouth to kiss a far more sensitive spot than her leg and grinned when she sucked in a sharp breath of air. "That's good, because I like Sparky better anyway...but you're assuming you'll be able to speak when I'm done."

His tongue and lips moved with an intent purpose and he was quickly rewarded with soft moans. Every sweat-covered dream and dirty fantasy he'd entertained couldn't compare to the sweetness of Jillian in reality.

This woman most definitely was going to be the death of him.

But what a perfect way to go.

***

Jillian

Present Day

Electric currents zinged along every nerve in her body. She had no idea Dean was a damned magician.

That was the only possible explanation for the near immediate surge of heat through her as he lavished attention on her aching core.

"What in the holy hell kind of classes did you wind up taking, Sparky?" She panted as her fingers dove into his hair, needing to keep him exactly where he was for just...just a few more...

He offered a gentle "mmmm" and the vibration was the final push to send her spiraling off the cliff of ecstasy. She couldn't even remember what she screamed, but she wasn't fully convinced there were any decipherable words.

He kissed up her abdomen, his tongue swirling inside her belly button as he went further north. His hands lagged his mouth and within moments dove between the trembling folds he'd so recently satiated.

She dug her nails into his shoulders. "Dean...I couldn't...not...I just..."

He grinned up at her before licking a circle around one of the hardened nipples. "You underestimate yourself, Jillybean." He wrapped his lips around the brown pebble and sucked. "And me. You definitely underestimate me."

Damn it all to hell if the bastard wasn't right. The attention he lavished on her chest and the mystical powers of the digits moving rapidly inside of her quickly reignited the blazing inferno of need that hadn't had a chance to burn out.

She clung to the same precipice again, simultaneously amazed at his ability and her body's response to him. She whimpered and pled for the relief she didn't possibly think she'd need so soon.

His tongue made a path from her chest to the column

of her neck and to her earlobe. He sucked lightly before moving his lips up and whispering softly, "Just let go, Jillybean."

Fireworks exploded behind her closed lids and she shrieked until her throat hurt. She almost thought she blacked out, the second pinnacle seemingly more intense than the first. She focused on trying to find something resembling a normal breath.

When she finally found the strength to open her eyes, she found herself face to face with his cocky ass grin. "Proud of yourself there, Sparky?"

His fingertips danced up her heated skin and sent a shiver through her entire being. "Pretty sure you've given me more than enough reason to be."

She lifted a brow and her own hand traveled down the front of him, slipping beneath the thin layer of material covering his hardened length. She clasped him in a firm grip and he groaned. "You've always been very, very good to me." She pushed on his chest until he fell onto his back and she straddled his waist. "But I prefer a more fifty/fifty arrangement."

"Such a giver." The words ended on a sharp inhale as her mouth repeated the actions he'd just performed on her only in reverse, moving from his throat, to his shoulders, down his chest...

She shoved his boxers down and tossed them behind her back. Her lips wrapped around the glistening tip of satiny flesh. Her hand stroked up and down the shaft.

"Damn, this is going to be a lightning round if you keep that shit up."

She lifted her head and looked at him, still gripping him firmly and moving at what she hoped was a maddeningly slow pace. She had a focused goal to pleasure him as much as he had her because...damn, that boy knew his stuff.

"What's the matter, Sparky? You can handle making a fire for me, but a little flame challenges your self-control?"

His deep groan turned into a guttural growl and he grabbed her biceps and turned, seamlessly moving her beneath him. "I am not too proud to admit you're driving me absolutely insane, but not just from touching me. Watching you fall apart was damn near a work of art."

Her thumping behind her ribcage had little to do with the renewed desire coursing through her veins and much more to do with Dean's words. Things that brought back the feelings she'd thought were permanently locked away in the recesses of her mind and heart, never to see the light of day again.

The immature childish crush that she'd briefly entertained in adolescence—and just as quickly banished thanks to a healthy and overwhelming fear Dean would go running for the hills at the mere suggestion—found new footing smack at the forefront of her brain.

Her lungs burned as her breathing shallowed. "Don't judge me."

The intensity of his stare melted into confusion. She wiggled beneath him enough to reach the drawer of the bedside stand. "I gave Angela the room card and...sent her on a mission for me earlier." She pulled out a strip of condoms and held them up for him as best as she could still on her back, pinned under his weight. "I might have been hoping you'd agree."

He grinned and took the foil packs from between her

fingers. "This is a good start, but we might need more than four."

Jillian's mouth immediately fell open. "More than four? What the hell did you get bitten by, a radioactive spider and gain superhuman abilities and manage to forget to tell me?"

Dean braced himself on his elbows over her and long moments passed with his gazing holding hers captive. The energy in the room shifted, or maybe she just imagined it, then he lowered himself enough to brush his lips along hers gently. Until she grabbed the back of his head and brought his mouth crashing into hers. Their tongues tangled and twisted together with desperation and need Jillian couldn't quite understand.

At least not in herself. She was pretty sure Dean had to be dying by this point.

She lifted her hips up to meet his in silent encouragement and his hand reached around to squeeze her ass and bring her even closer to him. He pulled back long enough to rip one of the foil packets between his teeth, but before he could don the condom, Jillian plucked it from his grasp. She flattened the palm of her other hand on his chest and once more pushed him onto his back.

She knelt over him, slowly rolling the latex into place before straddling him and lowering down at an agonizing pace.

Dean closed his eyes and arched his neck, pressing the back of his head into the pillow and giving a low moan. "You're trying to kill me, woman."

Jillian grinned and braced herself on his chest as she rocked her hips back and forth for a few minutes. "All part of my plan, Sparky."

He dug his fingers into her hips as he moved her up and down. "You have always been exceptionally successful at every plan you make."

A fresh wave of mounting need washed over her and the even plane she'd so briefly been on turned into a ninety degree ramp to the stars. Dean uttered a string of curses and his muscles tightened beneath her touch.

"Dammit, Jillian." He growled her name between clenched teeth and the very sound shot her into an entirely different stratosphere of pleasure right alongside him. She screamed his name. She screamed unintelligible words. But neither were anywhere close to being as loud as the internal declarations she couldn't deny in this moment.

Her dumb ass had gone and fallen in love with Dean Carlisle and had sex with him. Nothing in this world would ever be the same.

Chapter Twenty-Two

Dean

Nine Years Earlier

Dean scooped food into the last bowl and set it inside Gilligan's cage, giving the boxer mix a pat on the head and scratching behind his ear before closing the front gate. "Come on, Jilly, it is basically tradition by now, so you have to go with me."

She cuddled the small kitten she'd been playing with close one more time before gingerly replacing her in the cage and tossing in a handful of treats. "But it's your senior prom. The one you'll always remember. Don't you want to at least try to find a girlfriend to go with?"

"Girls are overrated." He dismissed her comment with a wave of his hand. "And besides, I'm going to have sorority chicks climbing all over me when I start college. I could use some time to rest up first."

Their weekly volunteer obligations at the humane society were usually a lot more fun, but Jillian had been giving him shit about what he thought was a no-brainer date to the prom. Ever since the homecoming dance last year that he had to take her to when Erica dumped his ass only a few weeks before the event, they'd simply gone to every school function at each of their schools together.

It was an unspoken pact that wasn't ever really discussed until this year, their senior year.

Jillian laid her hand across her abdomen, laughing loud enough to startle Gilligan and elicit a short bark before he returned his attention to the bowl in front of him. "Sorry, bud." She directed the comment to the dog before turning her full attention to Dean. "You too, if you're really that delusional."

Dean straightened himself to his full height that, as it always had, dwarfed her by nearly an entire foot. He straightened his arms and flexed a little. "Who wouldn't want a piece of this fine specimen of a man?" He threw her a wink. "Plus I am an expert on all that romantic bullshit girls like thanks to years of training from my best friend and trashy reality TV."

She plastered a sympathetic expression on her face. "Oh, I will gladly take all the credit for teaching you how to date two dozen women at a time equipped with nothing but red roses and an endless production budget."

"So, whaddaya say? Will you be my date for the senior prom?"

Jillian's gaze drifted around the room and she clasped her hands together, holding them close to her heart. "With an exceptionally romantic proposal like that, how could I possibly resist?"

He drew his brows together and stared at her for a long time, then scratched his head. "Is...that some weird way of saying yes?"

With a heaving sigh, she closed the few feet between them and patted his shoulder. "Yes, Sparky, that is a yes. And you're probably the densest human being ever."

"Hey, I resemble that remark."

They both said goodbye to the staff members at the shelter before they walked out the front door and headed to Dean's hand-me-down car that Connor passed on when he left for college. Freshman year he couldn't have a car on campus anyway and he'd been saving for a Jeep to take back with him for his second year.

He pulled open the passenger door for her as much out of the respect his mother had ingrained in all her boys as he did out of habit. "Up for some ice cream?"

Her emerald eyes glittered with excitement. "Do I ever turn down food?"

"No, never." He closed the door and jogged around the back of the car before climbing in the driver's seat and bringing the engine to life. "You need to marry a chef. No, wait, better yet, a farmer."

She laughed, snapping her belt into place. "Why's that, Sparky?"

"Because you always, always require food." He shifted into gear and slid seamlessly onto the highway. "And since you don't eat meat, a farmer would be absolutely perfect. All the vegetables you can eat, always ready."

She tilted her head and stared at him silently for

several moments. "Figured your plans out yet?"

It was a question he'd heard enough times—from Jillian, from his parents, from his brothers; hell, he was pretty sure the mailman had asked once or twice—that he should be immune to its effects. But still his stomach tightened. The simple answer was no.

The more complex answer was hell no and it was terrifying. All of his brothers were born with their futures clearly in view. His father built his own company from the ground up with no help just because it was his passion and he had a knack for it.

But Dean had no plan, no gifts, no overwhelming desire. He was certain most of the time that something was wrong with him because he didn't experience that all-consuming need to do one particular thing. How could he possibly be the only one of the entire Carlisle clan to be completely without a vision?

And Jillian's unwavering hunger to strike out for third world countries as soon as she graduated college only intensified the feelings of inferiority that plagued him when he tossed and turned in bed at nights. Thoughts he couldn't bring himself to tell anyone, not even Jillian.

"I'm going to declare something pretty basic to start with and get my crap classes out of the way. Like business administration or whatever. Then I'll figure out what I really want to do once I get there." It was the closest to a plan he could come up with.

He pulled into one of the parking spaces right in front of the small ice cream stand. Before they got out, Jillian laid a hand on top of his where it rested on the gearshift. He forced his gaze to meet hers, slightly fearful the judgment and condemnation he heaped on himself would be reflected back at him.

But he really should have trusted her more.

She gave his fingers a quick tight squeeze. "I think that's a perfect plan for you, Sparky." She opened the door and hopped out of her seat. "By the way, you're buying and I'm totally getting three scoops."

***

Jillian

Nine Years Earlier

Before Dean even had a chance to fully open the front door, she launched herself in his arms. As soon as she read the letter there was no one else she wanted to tell. She'd raced out of her house, through the backyard, beside Fredrock, making sure to run her hand across the surface for good luck, and up the cement stairs at the front of his house. No matter how many times his mother had told her to just walk right in, she always knocked.

"I got in!" She shrieked the handful of words as she squeezed his neck and the paper tighter. "I got in, I got in, I got in!"

He held her firmly against him and spun around in circles in the middle of the entryway. "Hot damn, I knew you would. Congrats, Jillybean."

His parents emerged from one of the rooms near the back of the house, frowns firmly in place until the scene before them registered and their faces immediately morphed into amusement. In the half a second before Dean lowered her to the ground, she noted the older couple's hands linked together and a mixture of jealousy and longing swept through her.

The affection his parents openly displayed toward one another and their children was like nothing she'd seen in her own.

A small smile tugged at her lips. Her grandparents, on the other hand, acted like newlyweds until her grandmother passed a few years earlier.

It was the exact kind of marriage she wanted for herself and for her children to see. Someday.

She banished the romantic ideations and held up the now wrinkled paper for display. "I got into Georgia State University. It's one of the top schools for nonprofit management and they took me!"

His parents each offered congratulatory hugs and kisses. Mike Carlisle flicked his wrist and offered the same suspiciously mischievous grin his son sported way too often. "Looks like you came just in time for dinner. Where do you want to go to celebrate?"

"A field." Dean piped up from behind her. "Something with lots of grass and dandelions so she can graze for hours."

Jillian spun on one heel, propped her fists on her hips and glared at him. "Are you making fun of me because I'm vegetarian? Because I don't want to eat living, breathing, adorable animals? Because I think that they are treated inhumanely and that we as smart, ingenuitive beings could do better?"

He blinked several times in rapid succession, his face completely void of all emotion. "Yes. Yes, I am."

She looked back at his parents over her shoulder. "Do we really have to take him to dinner with us? It would be so much more enjoyable without," she waved a hand up and down to encompass his six foot plus self, "that."

The two adults laughed. Dean's father grabbed his keys from the hook by the door and pulled his and his wife's lightweight jackets from the adjacent closet.

Dean slung an arm over Jillian's shoulders and steered her toward the exit that led to the garage. "You'd miss me."

Three simple words he meant as a joke hit her in a funny way. She would absolutely miss him like crazy. Her grandfather, Henry, Frieda, and Dean. A small, but loyal group of people she knew loved her beyond a shadow of a doubt, even if she was the odd child who dressed like a hippie and took up unwinnable causes.

For the first time since she opened the letter and was overcome with total elation, her heart plummeted to her toes. Before climbing inside the back of the SUV as Dean held the door for her, she turned and wrapped her arms tight around his neck, forcing him to bend at the waist to avoid being choked.

"I will," she whispered in his ear. "I will miss you so much."

He pulled back and offered a cocky smirk. "Not a chance in hell you will. I'll be driving down far too often for you to even have a chance to miss me."

Chapter Twenty-Three

Dean

Present Day

He lay in the bed staring at the darkness created by his closed eyes, afraid to open them and be confronted with the possibility that last night was all an exceptionally realistic dream. When he finally peeped through barely parted lids, the mass of ginger waves splayed across his chest eased the band of tension that barely allowed him to breathe.

She moved slightly and he held every cell in his body at rigid attention until she stilled. When the soft puffs of air from her nose blew against his abdomen in a gentle, steady rhythm, he allowed himself to relax and commit every miniscule detail to memory.

This was a dream come true and an epic nightmare all rolled into one.

Damn it all to hell, he wished he could just grow a set and tell her that this wasn't a fake marriage to him and he'd do anything if she'd give him a chance to prove he really loved her. Everything he should have said before falling into bed with her.

His thumb stroked along her bicep to her shoulder and back down. The reality of Jillian in his arms asking, offering... he was a weak man when it came to her and that was just reinforced last night.

She wasn't lying. He'd seen her in a bikini every summer for years. He'd touched her, held her, hell, they'd even kissed when they were kids. But none of that mattered. Every caress, every kiss was completely different. Not only because she was naked, because that sure as hell helped, but because he had the chance to pour every drop of his emotion into the actions.

Jillian stirred beside him again, this time picking up her head and offering a sleepy smile. Just before the color drained from her face and she scooted back on the bed, clutching the designer sheets to her chest. "I..."

Dean sat up, his arm shot out to grab her arm. "Don't." If she said she was sorry, if she said she regretted it, he wasn't sure his heart could handle being shredded that deeply.

Her pale complexion regained its ivory tone and then morphed into a crimson shade. She shook her head slightly. "I loved last night. I just..." She gripped his hand in both of hers and finally brought her eyes up to meet his. "Promise me that nothing will change. Dealing with all this shit with my family has just...I need to know that I will always have my best friend. No matter what."

She had the power to rip him in half with only a few

words. But she was also the only person who could somehow stitch him back together.

"I'm not going anywhere." Even to his own ears, his tone was slightly more vehement than he'd intended. He tempered the statement with as cocky of a smirk as he could possibly muster. "Plus you made a damn good argument to the whole 'friends with benefits' thing. Keep that shit up and Tanner is going to hire you."

She rolled her eyes and stress he didn't even know he was holding evaporated from his shoulders. Everything was back to normal and he was annoying her as much as ever.

Dean bit the inside of his cheek, wanting to see exactly how far he could push it. And how much temptation he could endure before he picked her up and carried her into the shower with him. "Go get a shower. We've got a full schedule."

Which was probably a mistake of the most epic proportions when she shot him a challenging glare and stood, the sheet falling from her body and taking all the oxygen in his lungs with it.

"Sure thing, Sparky."

Even if he tried there wasn't a chance in hell he could stop his eyes from tracking every sway of her hips and perfectly round ass as she walked away with more confidence than should legally be allowed. As soon as the door clicked closed behind her he flopped back against the pillows and scrubbed his eyes with a groan.

What in the hell was he doing?

He sprung up from the mattress and snagged the boxers that somehow were hanging from the lamp on the dresser on the opposite side of the room. He slid them on, needing a barrier of some kind in place so he didn't run into the shower and join her. The water spray echoing from the luxurious bathroom was tempting as hell. Especially when his mind began creating images of drops tracking from one delicious little freckle to the next.

He grabbed the suitcase that was still sitting right beside the door where he'd dropped it last night and plopped it onto the sofa in the living area of the suite. The room seemed like a waste for one night, but Georgia had insisted they needed at least some time away.

And then promptly berated her husband for expecting Dean back at work Monday morning.

He rooted through the luggage until he located the jeans and casual shirt he'd packed. An irrepressible grin took over his face. This sort of "honeymoon" would probably be shot down by ninety percent of women, but it would be something Jillian would love.

Dean balled up his clothes and tucked them under his arm, resting his shoulder on the frame, waiting for Jillian to appear. She pulled the door open and jumped slightly, resting a hand on her chest, bare above the knot holding the towel wrapped around her.

He quirked a brow with a blatantly mischievous smirk, his gaze traveling up and down her barely covered body. Crossing that line with Jillian was either the smartest or stupidest decision of his life.

She smacked his upper arm and crossed the room to fish out clothes from the suitcase he'd left open on the chair. "You're impossible."

Dean just laughed and whistled a random tune as he closed himself in the bathroom. Somehow the steamy space managed to retain the light, airy citrus scent that defined Jillian despite her use of the hotel provided body wash.

He forced his mind to anything but her as he scrubbed himself clean and quickly dressed. He had a plan and he was impatient as hell to put it into action.

By the time he emerged from the bathroom, she was dressed in denim capris and a white top with blue and mauve stitching and cut out shoulders. It was the quintessential bohemian look she'd mastered early into her freshman year of college.

"Ready to go, Mrs. Monroe-Carlisle?" Maybe a little cheesy, maybe a little pathetic, but he really liked how that sounded.

Jillian tilted her head to the side and her gaze went from amused to stormy to something he couldn't read in under five seconds. "What exactly do you have planned?"

He grabbed the suitcase from the chair with one hand and snaked the other arm around her waist pulling her firmly against his body. "If there is one benefit to fake marrying your best friend, it's that he will for real know exactly how to show you a good time."

***

Jillian

Present Day

The naked gray building looked more like a warehouse than anything else and gave Jillian exactly zero clues about what was contained inside. She tilted her head and gave Dean a quizzical look as he threw his tiny sports car into park. She had been fairly impressed that the car his parents had bought for him as a graduation gift remained as spotless and immaculate as it had when it left the showroom floor.

As always, Dean knew her better than anyone else and immediately responded to her unasked question. He turned slightly in his seat to face her. "You keep talking about all the things I'm giving up because of this." He gestured back and forth between them. "But I know you and I know that being in one place, being stuck in my townhouse with nothing to do is probably going to kill you."

She dropped her gaze to her lap and fidgeted with the hem of her shirt. "It's more complicated than what I want."

Dean hooked a finger under her chin forcing her to look him in the eye. "What you want is my top priority."

A wave of emotion washed over her, the realization last night that the feelings she'd had in high school resurfaced and were far stronger than before still so fresh and leaving her already aching heart raw. He had no idea the impact of those few words.

She swallowed back the lump that had formed so quickly in her throat and put on a smile she hoped appeared far more carefree than it actually was. "You're aiming for BFF of the year aren't you, Sparky?"

He winked and smirked, then climbed out of the car before answering. In the handful of seconds it took him to round the hood she closed her eyes and took a deep, calming breath. Having sex with Dean might have been the biggest mistake she ever made. With damn near anyone else she could have fallen into a friends with benefits relationship easily. It made sense for her in nearly every aspect.

But Dean was the one person it couldn't happen with and she should have known better than to try.

Before she was ready, he yanked open the door and held out a hand to help her out of the low riding vehicle. "I'm pretty sure I've had that particular award in the bag for at least twenty years."

He laced his fingers through hers and tugged her toward the glass front door. If she tried, she wasn't sure she could count the number of times they'd held hands, but deep within herself she noticed a change. One she was positive was one-sided, but present nonetheless.

And in that moment she wasn't sure she could survive the end of their supposedly fake marriage that was currently far too real.

"So, what's the plan here, Sparky?"

He opened the door, released his grip on her, and rested his hand lightly on her lower back as he entered the room a step behind her. "You'll see."

She pressed her lips together, her eyes darting around the space to try to solve the mystery in her head.

An older man with a receding hairline and expanding waistline approached them with a wide grin and stuck out a large paw toward Dean. "Hey, you did come."

Dean shook the other man's hand in a brief shake. "I told you we were coming."

"I didn't think you were actually serious about that. Who the hell shows up at a place like this the day after they get married?"

Dean looked down at Jillian, put an arm around her

waist, and pulled her close to his side, her body fitting his perfectly and her heart shredding just a little more. "We aren't your normal, average couple, are we, Jillybean?"

We aren't a couple at all, although I am fairly certain I would give damn near anything to make this real right now.

The vehemence of the thought even shocked her and she struggled to paste a nonchalant smile on her face. For once she was grateful for cotillion and etiquette classes and the ceaseless lectures from her mother to always put on a happy, genial face, no matter how much she was dying inside.

As much as she could, she ignored the storm of emotions raging havoc in her and dutifully followed the man, whose name she still didn't know, and Dean as they led her behind a set of heavy metal security doors.

"So Jillian," the man said as he led them down a corridor, "you ought to know that Dean brags about your work with Doctors Without Borders all the time."

She nodded and some of the turmoil swirling inside her settled. Her work was something she loved, something she was passionate about, and was far more than a simple career choice. She believed with every iota of her being that this was her purpose in life, helping people by actually helping and not slapping a sad picture on a fundraising poster. Although, shortly after she began working, she gained a measure of gratitude for what her mother did. Funding was definitely always needed.

Dean was right. Staying at home for the next eighteen months might kill her.

She looked up at Dean as the man turned to the left

and pushed open another set of doors. "You two have known each other for a while?"

A small smile curled Dean's lips as they all stopped just inside the large room. "I've changed a bit while you were gone." His voice was soft, and it was as if they were cocooned in their own small world. "Sam and I have worked together for a couple of years now."

"Dean has been a huge help in working with some of our people and helping us get started." Sam—she was grateful to finally know his name, but annoyed when his voice cut through, breaking the magic spell that had descended over them. He held an arm out and turned in a half circle, encompassing the entire room in one sweeping gesture.

Jillian drew her brows together as she took in the mountains of medical supplies piled on tables around the periphery of the expansive space. Her gaze darted from the massive hoard to Sam, and then finally rested on Dean. "I don't understand…"

Her best friend, who lately she was feeling as though she might not even know anymore, laughed lightly. "I figured for a girl like you, there would be no better honeymoon activity than helping out at Sam's community outreach."

Dean led her to the various tables stocked with syringes and masks and gloves. "Sam and a couple of other doctors in the area have begun a privately funded and privately owned project to help provide those who are homeless or low income with free vaccinations and some basic supplies to protect them while they are out."

The other man nodded, a shadow of concern crossing his face. "The state has clinics set up for people to go to, but not everyone feels comfortable in a government run setting. Some avoid being on the radar like the plague. Here we don't ask for real names or any form of ID. We keep track of who is who on our own, but we just offer safety and help."

He grabbed her hand and led her from the room into the next one through an adjoining door. "We also have coats and blankets and sleeping bags."

His excitement was nearly palpable and so very contagious as he took her down the hall into a huge kitchen that she couldn't help but giggle. "And we have dinner every night as well as some bags of food to take with them like juice and granola bars and…what is that look for?"

Heedless of the warning sirens blaring in her brain telling her that this was a very bad idea, she grabbed his face between her hands and planted a firm kiss on his lips. "Dean Carlisle, you might have just won husband of the year as well."

Chapter Twenty-Four

Dean

Nine Years Earlier

Dean skipped a rock across the pond. Then he kicked a clump of grass. Then he pulled a few random weeds out.

"How long can a graduation possibly be?" He muttered the question into the empty space around him with a grunt. He was still annoyed that Jillian only was allowed to have four guests at her graduation and every spot had been claimed by her parents, brother, and grandfather.

He sank down onto Fredrock and turned his attention back to her house in the distance, hoping to see any sign of movement that she was home. Waiting was most definitely not his strong suit.

Finally after nothing short of an eternity had passed,

the back door of her house slid open and Jillian sprinted across the lawn toward their spot—still wearing her cap and gown, a fact he found incredibly amusing. Even more so when she had to hold a hand on the hat to keep it from flying off as she ran.

Dean stood and opened his arms, catching her in a firm bear hug. "You did it, Jilly!"

She pushed back on his shoulders slightly so she could look him in the eye. "I did! And I didn't throw up or run away either, so that is a total win."

With a deep chuckle, Dean lowered her back down onto her feet. "Definitely counts as a win to have a vomit-less graduation ceremony." He stood back and eyed her up and down. "I thought your parents were taking you out to dinner after the graduation. Why are you still wearing all that?"

She ducked her head and looked up at him through her lashes. "You couldn't be there and I wanted you to see me, so I put it back on." Her fingers traced the lettering on the gold stole around her neck that declared her Valedictorian status in bold, black letters.

"Oh!" She hiked up the skirt of her robe and fished around in the hidden pocket of the white dress she wore beneath it. She entered her passcode into her phone and held it out to him. "Brad recorded my speech for me. Want to watch?"

He took the device with a broad smile and sat down on Fredrock, patting the smooth stone beside him. "This definitely classifies as must see TV."

Jillian grinned back at him and took a seat beside him, drawing her legs up so her knees pressed into her chest. "All you're missing is the popcorn."

"I'm good like this." Dean put an arm around her

shoulders and pulled her close to him, holding the device out so they could both watch. "Now hush, this is rumored to be the speech of the century."

Resting her forearms on her knees, she shook her head. "Not even close there, Sparky."

The images on the screen blurred and then the audio cut out. Jillian gasped and grabbed the phone from him. She turned it on and off then did a hard reboot. "No, no, no, no, no." She looked up at him, the corners of her eyes glittering from unshed tears. "It's not working. What the hell did he do wrong?"

Jillian mad was entertaining. Jillian sarcastic usually meant she was cracking jokes at his expense. Jillian passionate was a work of art.

But Jillian on the verge of tears was Dean's only weakness.

"Hey." He hooked a finger under her chin and brought her eyes up from the device she clutched so tightly he was sure she'd crack the glass screen to meet his. "Why would I want to watch a video anyway when I have the real thing live and in person?"

Her mouth fell open and she shook her head. "I can't...here?"

Dean held a hand out to her and helped her stand up on Fredrock. "Take it away, Ms. Monroe. You have a completely captive audience of one." He winked. "But don't take too long, I don't have popcorn and I'm starting to get hungry."

Jillian's eyes lit up. "Ice cream?"

He groaned and smacked the heel of his palm to his forehead. "Fine, I'll feed your never ending appetite *after* you deliver your valedictorian speech."

The sun began setting just over her shoulder as she

spoke, kissing her red hair with the fading light and creating a natural spotlight behind her. She fidgeted with her stole as she started speaking, but soon fell into a natural rhythm and delivered every word with passion and conviction.

Two things that defined her life.

And two things Dean couldn't manage to discover about anything other than his best friend. Their relationship was the most precious thing in the world to him and he'd protect it with everything he had.

***

Jillian

Nine Years Earlier

"Dean Carlisle."

As soon as the superintendent called out his name, Jillian leapt to her feet, screaming and cheering, clapping until her palms stung. She was certain he couldn't hear her with his parents, brothers, and sister-in-law all just as loud, but she loved being able to show how proud she was of him.

After the ceremony closed, she ducked and pushed her way through the crowd until she located Dean and promptly launched herself into his arms.

"Sparky, I am *so* proud of you!" She squeezed his neck tight and gave a small squeal in his ear.

He held onto her tightly for a moment before setting her onto her feet. "Yeah, well, I wasn't top of the class like *some* people, Miss Valedictorian."

Jillian rolled her eyes. "It's a pointless title that

means absolutely nothing."

"Hey, Deano." Some guy with sandy blond hair walked up to them, clasped one of Dean's hands in his and patted Dean on the back with the other one. "We survived." His gaze landed on Jillian and they lit up with appreciation. "This your girlfriend?"

She opened her mouth to correct the other man, but Dean draped an arm around her shoulders and pulled her close to his side before she could speak.

"Yeah, it is. And we have plans so I have to go, but I'll catch you around, Tyler." With that Dean steered her away from the crowd toward where his parents and siblings stood.

Jillian stood back for a moment as they all hugged and congratulated him. Dean's immediate declaration that she was his girlfriend was confusing and unsettling.

And reignited the want deep inside that she was desperately trying to ignore.

He broke away from his family and grabbed her hand. "We're going to meet them at the restaurant."

She looked over at him out of the corner of her eye as they wove through throngs of people to find their way to the parking lot and, eventually, located his car. She kept her mouth shut until they were both inside and buckled and stuck in a line of traffic.

"So want to clue me in on what that was all about?"

Dean drew his brows together and frowned at her. "What was what about?"

Jillian offered a strangled laugh. "The whole "yeah, this is my girlfriend" bit? I mean, I'm not saying I'm not flattered, Sparky, but that's usually something you ask the girl about first rather than just deciding on your own."

He rolled his eyes. "Look, I like Tyler, but he's a jerk. He's seen us at the dance, so it was a reasonable point to make." He rested his wrist on the steering wheel and looked over at her. "He'd hound me for your number and quite possibly follow us to dinner."

A brief moment of hope flared in her chest. If Dean was that concerned then maybe...

"Only you and I know how ridiculous that is. Everyone else could easily picture us madly in love." He maneuvered the car through the vehicles parked on either side creating a small ally to exit.

The flame flickered and died. The lead weight of reality sunk to the pit of her stomach. Her smile, thankfully, slipped easily into place. "Right? You and I would be like *War of the Roses*, only worse."

He shot her a lopsided grin before shifting gears and gunning the engine as he finally broke free of the barely moving line of vehicles and found a stretch of wide, open road. "More like *Mr. and Mrs. Smith*."

Jillian nudged his bicep with her elbow. "Are you secretly an assassin trying to kill me?"

Dean let out a short bark of laughter. "Nah, but the chemistry on that one was hot as hell." He puffed out his chest. "And you gotta admit with a fine specimen such as myself it would be damn near impossible for you to keep your hands off me if we were living together."

"Oh, yes." She clasped both hands together over her heart and gave a deep sigh. "It's a struggle I face all the time. I barely restrain myself from jumping your bones on a daily basis."

He clucked his tongue. "Now, now, Ms. Monroe, whatever would the Ice Queen and her merry band of loyal yes women say if they heard you talking that way?"

Jillian groaned and sank deeper into the seat closing her eyes. "I wish I had the guts to find out."

Dean reached over and grabbed one of her hands, lacing his fingers through hers and pulling it so they rested on the center console. "Look on the bright side, in three months you'll be two hundred and eleven miles away from the Glass Castle and the Ice Queen's rule."

She rotated her head and lifted one lid to look at him. "You counted?"

"Hell, yeah," he tightened his grip on her slightly. "Gotta figure out the fastest route in case I need to kick some frat boy's ass."

Jillian laughed lightly and some of the stormy emotions inside settled. No matter what he'd be her best friend and that was what mattered the most.

Chapter Twenty-Five

Dean

Present Day

He may be twenty-seven, a partner in a successful business, and—as far as everyone on the outside of their marriage was concerned—son-in-law to the great and powerful Monroe family, but he still hated standing outside of the imposing monstrosity Jillian called home.

An involuntary smile pulled at his lips. Not anymore. Home was his house, with him. And he'd do anything to keep it that way. But first...

The door swung wide in front of him and Henry's stoic veneer cracked for a fleeting moment when he saw Dean standing on the other side. All too soon the older man composed his features into the same cold, professional expression he always wore. He bent slightly at the waist. "Good morning, Mr. Carlisle. May

I ask why you're calling?"

Over their twenty years of friendship, it never failed to amuse him how different their lives were. And the fact that Jillian basically grew up in the kind of home that he once thought only lived on in movies or books. "Hey there, Henry. Is Mr. Monroe available?"

Henry merely nodded and stood to the side, holding an arm out for Dean to come in.

Dutifully, Dean followed the older man down the hallway, and every memory of his brief and infrequent visits here played through his mind. He knew the massive house well enough to know they were heading exactly where he expected, to Edward Monroe's study.

Henry knocked twice, and at the grunted "come in" that filtered through the door, he opened the thick oak plank and gestured for Dean to enter.

Edward held his forehead in one hand, his elbow propped on the ornate wooden desk. "Henry, I need to speak with—Dean? What are you doing here?" The older man stood. "Is something wrong with Jillian?"

Dean immediately shook his head. "Not...not like that. May I sit, sir?" Although she may have had four rowdy boys to corral, and probably let them get away with more than they deserved far too often, manners were one thing Tracy Carlisle insisted upon. And he knew better than to allow them to slip in this household.

There were probably ghosts of genteel ladies and refined men waiting in the wings to pounce if he dared step out of line. A shiver ran down his spine. He really did hate this place.

Edward nodded and then lowered himself back into the leather chair. "Then why are you here?"

Dean glanced over his shoulder as he took a seat on

the opposite side of the desk, making sure they were alone. "First, I want you to understand that I say this with all due respect, but I am also here because of Jilly." The tight band around his heart constricted at the mere mention of her name. Damn, he was hopeless.

Jillian's father frowned at him, his thick, bushy, gray brows drawn tightly together. "So far I don't like where this conversation is going."

A war of emotions raged inside of him from contempt for the man who created a situation that caused Jillian even a moment of stress, to empathy and understanding, to a rather overwhelming urge to deck the guy.

Instead he cleared his throat. "Sir, Jillian told me everything. I knew about the will before the wedding, but she also explained why it was so important." He left out the tiny detail that she was completely shit-faced when she made the confession.

Edward's face turned an ugly shade of red. "So, that's what this is about? You're married to my daughter for two days and you think you have the dirt and the power to bring the hundreds of years of our family's legacy to its knees by exposing us or forcing us to give you part of the trust?"

Anger and distrust and projection were all reactions he was used to, but the difference this time was they carried with them the implication that Dean would even entertain the idea of doing something to hurt Jillian.

Hell to the no on that one.

He took a deep breath and pushed down the frustration and irritation inside. He held up both hands, palms out. "That isn't what I said at all. In fact, I am completely in favor of keeping this quiet because Jillian

223

doesn't need any more stress than what you've already given her."

Her father's once mottled face drained of all its color. He dropped his head. "Then what the hell do you want? My gratitude?"

"I want to help you." It was partially true. He wanted to help the other man—but not for him, for Jillian. Despite her family's total lack of support for her career and life choices, he knew she carried the weight of obligation and loyalty. She was devoted to the people and the legacy, not only because of them, but because of her grandfather.

Edward turned in his seat, grabbed a decanter from the shelves lining the wall behind him, and filled the crystal glass on his desk with the rich amber liquid. "Exactly what kind of help are you offering, young man?"

Dean shifted slightly in his seat. He probably should have talked to Jillian before this, and he definitely should have clued her in to all the things he did on the ranch, but he was nearly certain she'd brush him off. And he knew deep down that this would be the best option for the entire family. "Do you know what I do? As a career, I mean."

The older man took a long drink, nearly draining the glass in one gulp. He set the nearly empty crystal down on the desk softly and gave a sharp shake of his head. "No, can't say I do."

Dean smiled, this was definitely his comfort zone. He may have spent far more years than he cared to admit floundering around for his purpose in life, but now that he'd discovered it, he loved to talk about nothing more.

He made a mental note to actually talk about it to his wife. And soon.

"I run a program with my cousin Mat at my brother's ranch. He's a psychologist that is trained in helping those who are recovering with addiction. We utilize equine therapy as part of their rehabilitation process." Dean leaned forward in his chair slightly. "We have worked with a wide variety of addictions including drugs, alcohol…and gambling."

Edward's eyes widened, but he stayed silent and Dean took that as an encouraging sign.

"I've already told you that Jillian explained everything to me and I know all too well that admitting you have a problem is the hardest and biggest step, but your addiction has gotten to a point where your family was in jeopardy. Your home was in jeopardy. Hundreds of years of the legacy you are so proud of was in jeopardy."

He rested his elbows on his knees and clasped his hands together. "I came here to invite you to RA Ranch and join us. There is no judgment, only an offer of help." He swallowed down the inexplicable lump that formed in his throat. "Please, consider the option."

Silence took over the room as he ended his short, but familiar speech, slightly modified each time he gave it. The only sounds beside their breathing that filled the large space was the tinkling of the ice on the crystal as Edward swirled his cup.

Dean stood and rubbed his palms down the thighs of his jeans. "Thank you for giving me the time to talk to you."

With that he crossed the room, knowing from experience that it would take time before someone as

225

proud as Edward Monroe was ready to face his failures and admit he needed help.

Just as his hand landed on the finely etched iron handle, Edward called out to him. "Dean, wait."

He turned slightly and looked at the older man over his shoulder, brows lifted in question.

"I…" Edward stood, resting his fingertips on his desk. "Can you tell me more about your program?"

***

Jillian

Present Day

Jillian topped off Angela's glass and set the wine bottle on the coffee table as she folded a leg beneath her and dropped down onto the couch beside her friend. "You just got here. It sucks you're leaving again."

The other woman took a long draw from her glass. "Don't you have a husband that you need to give some attention to? He couldn't have been happy to have me here cramping your style and forcing you two to keep it down last night."

Heat pooled near her collarbone and crept up her neck. With their guest sleeping a few feet away on the sofa, nothing happened that required intentional silence. However…

An avalanche of dirty and delicious memories from their wedding night cascaded through her mind and caused a knot of desire to form low in her belly.

She was a damn fool to suggest they try out the whole "friends with benefits" bullshit. She loved him.

As much as she tried to deny it since the realization first hit in high school, she still did.

Taking their relationship to that level of intimacy once was stupid. Flames of condemnation slowly moved closer to her cheekbones. Twice was idiocy. Desire dried every drop of moisture from her mouth. But the third time they'd had sex that night was totally on Dean. He'd woken her from a deep, dreamless sleep with his lips on her neck and...

Holy hell, she was hopeless.

"Dean and I..." Her words trailed off and she quickly downed a large gulp of the red wine. "Things are different for us. I can guarantee you that he didn't utter a single complaint about having you stay here."

Angela set her now empty glass on the coffee table. "Different and boring are not synonymous. Why the hell didn't you two take a decent honeymoon?"

Because it was a fake wedding and it's a fake marriage and the only real thing that will come of this is my completely and totally shattered heart. Oh yeah, and my super proper southern family is the reason this all happened so I could save them from ruin and rejection.

She wasn't certain if it was the nearly empty third glass of wine or desperation to let out all the half-truths and deception she resented carrying, but the truth danced dangerously close to the tip of her tongue, threatening to be spoken any second.

"We've known each other forever." She offered with a small shrug. "Our marriage came from twenty years of friendship."

Angela pulled her legs up on the sofa and wrapped her arms around them, hugging her knees to her chest.

"Mmm, and is there any specific reason why you failed to mention that your bestie was hotter than Hades in summer?"

Jillian tipped the wineglass back and the last drops of the sweet crimson liquid slid down her throat. "Possibly because I spent many, many years of that friendship pointedly ignoring that small detail." She set the crystal on the coffee table beside the bottle and mirrored Angela's position. "Do you have any idea how miserable it is to be seventeen and madly in love with your best friend who basically can't see you as anything even resembling a real girl?"

Angela laughed and grabbed a throw pillow, tucking it between her head and the back of the couch as she pushed a few errant dark curls behind her ear. "I'm sure he outgrew that phase pretty quick. That boy is devoted to you."

She sighed and stared out the front window in the fading light of the evening. Arguing with Angela was pointless and would only end in her heart aching even more.

In some ways, she was right. Dean *was* devoted, and that was never more evident than when he agreed to give up nearly two years of his life for her.

But none of that translated to Dean loving her the way she'd always dreamt, giving her the kind of marriage his parents had and her grandparents had. It just meant that she would need to fall back on all the years of etiquette training and pretend to be fine for as long as it took for her to land another assignment and run as far away as she could to lick her wounds.

And even though she may live to regret it, right now she would greedily take every second she had with him and hope the memories would comfort her rather than destroy her when she tried to rebuild her life.

She ground her molars together and questioned if her family was truly worth this in the end.

Just as quickly as the thought popped into her head, it was answered as an image of her grandfather floated through her mind and reaffirmed her decision. He was so proud of all their family had done over the years and was proud of *her*. Something her mother and father never had been.

So she would suck it up and be the adult she needed to be to get through this. And she'd take every moment of their carefully crafted deeply in love public persona as well as their private friends-with-benefits arrangement and imprint it on her brain to pull out on the lonely nights when she'd attempt to sleep under a mosquito net in the bush. Because that would be the only way she could possibly survive.

A single bright headlight and loud, roaring engine cut through the dark thoughts plaguing her mind and her aching heart immediately thumped back to life. Dean was home. She fought the urge to run and greet him at the door, fairly certain that would be overkill even for the couple pretending to be entwined in wedded bliss.

She caught the clock on the far wall just as the doorknob turned. It was after seven and the damn little voice of darkness taunted her with the idea that he stayed away longer than needed to avoid coming home. Regretting everything from the wedding to the sex.

His face was a little drawn, but his countenance brightened as soon as he caught sight of her and a measure of the weight bearing down on her shoulders lifted. He crossed the few feet separating them and dropped a kiss on the top of her head. A perfectly normal act for newlyweds. "Honey, I'm home."

Jillian patted the day's worth of facial hair growing along his jawline. "My hero, bringing home the bacon for his little lady."

"Soy bacon," he corrected as he disappeared behind the kitchen cabinets. "Did you guys eat yet?"

Angela held up the empty wine bottle and popcorn bowl. "Does this count?"

Dean poked his head out and lifted a single brow. "Okay, are you two making up for Georgia being out of commission? Popcorn and wine are her designated meals of choice, not yours. I'll make...something."

Jillian popped off the couch and followed him into the kitchen, pulling him deeper into the small space, away from Angela's prying eyes. She scanned his face closer, taking in the dark circles under his lower lids. She cupped his cheeks in her hands. "You look exhausted."

"I am. And my head is killing me." He leaned into her touch and her heart ached with desire to care for him. "I had a new client today and...it was a bit more than I expected."

The comment served as a reminder to ask for more detail about his job. Later.

She gave him a tight hug that was far briefer and far more friendly than she wanted and spun him around on his feet, facing him toward the hallway and his bedroom door. "To bed now. Angela and I are perfectly capable of feeding ourselves."

He took a few steps away then turned back to her. "And you promise it'll be something more than popcorn and wine?"

Jillian stuck her tongue out and her middle finger up. "Keep up those smartass comments and you'll wake up to find your hand in a bowl of warm water."

Dean glanced into living room and made a face at Angela. "Clearly cotillion classes worked wonders on my wife."

He made his way to the bedroom and her heart tumbled to the floor. How in the hell did two words like "my wife" manage to bring such joy and pain at the exact same time?

Chapter Twenty-Six

Dean

Present Day

He pulled the bike to a stop in front of his townhome, threw the kickstand down, and stood, taking off his helmet and holding it under his arm as he jogged up the steps and unlocked the front door. They'd quickly fallen into an easy routine over the past week and a half and damned if he didn't find himself loving it.

Dean hung his helmet from the large hook Jillian had installed while he'd been at work because she was tired of seeing it on the floor. A small smile tugged at his lips. Apparently the fourth time she'd stubbed her toe on it had been the final straw.

He tugged open the door that led to the basement and the integral garage and descended a few steps to peek around the corner. Jillian had been taking his tiny sportscar every day to work with Sam's community outreach project and she loved every minute.

Especially driving the fiery red car that had a tendency to entice even the most cautious driver to test the power of its engine.

He pulled a box of the dry plant-based faux chicken from the cabinet and added water and oil so he could form it into what he hoped would look like chicken strips. Earlier in the week Jillian had mentioned wanting chicken Caesar wraps and he'd stored the information away to make for dinner at some point.

He was far from a culinary genius, but he managed to feed himself real food ever since he'd graduated college and found his own place, and he hadn't poisoned himself in the process.

Dean whistled lightly as he put the "tastes like chicken" strips in the oven to bake. He'd resolved himself to taking Jillian on a special date this weekend and talking to her about everything. Certainly the past ten days of wedded bliss and heated nights had to convince her that he was all in for real, not just for a while.

Something he should have done a while ago, but he just…wanted the chance to show her just how good it could be if she was willing to take a chance on them.

He pulled two plates down from the cabinet just as the door leading to the garage latched closed. "Hey, Jilly," he called out. "I'm making dinner."

She hung her purse on yet another set of hooks she'd installed, this time by the basement entrance. "It smells good." She leaned her rear end against the counter and drew her lips in between her teeth. "I need to talk to you about something."

The heat from the oven as he opened the door had him blinking against the steam. He took the pan that held the strips out and set it on top of the stove. "That sounds a bit ominous."

Distress etched itself in her features and she crossed her arms in front of her. "Sam offered me a job."

His heart thumped harder behind his breastbone. It was like he was receiving a gift he'd never asked for, but desperately needed. Part of what he loved most about Jillian was her endless drive to help as many people as she could. It was also something he worried about most.

"You don't look very happy about that. Most people are thrilled by a job offer." He tried his damnedest to keep his tone light, but he also knew that she knew him well enough to hear everything he didn't want her to.

She sighed and took the plate he offered her filled with kettle-cooked potato chips and the Caesar chicken wrap and took her seat at the table. "It's not that. It's...it's a great job and I've only been there a few days, but it is an amazing program."

He nodded and mirrored her actions, sitting to her right. "Yeah, we were pretty fortunate to get so much help from the medical community. Tons of doctors and nurses have been willing to donate time and supplies and it's made a huge difference."

Jillian chewed one of the chips slowly and stared at him. "You've never actually answered any of my questions on how you know Sam." She took a long drink of her water. "Or the ones where I ask exactly what the hell it is you do for Wyatt. If I didn't know better, I'd think it was a government conspiracy."

234

"Don't worry, Jillybean, I'm not an assassin and I have no plans to take you out." He winked and was rewarded with her grin in response.

The truth was telling her about the program he started with Mat was part of the whole declaring his love for her thing. She was the reason he'd started it, she was the reason he'd finally found his purpose, she was the driving force for everything. And she had no idea.

Her faith in him, her gentle encouragement, and her unwavering support when he was drowning in a sea of uncertainty and doubt were exactly what he needed. And they all combined to give him the confidence to pursue something more meaningful with his life.

He loved her in so many ways and just needed to grow a spine and say it.

"Dean, I get that this marriage isn't real—and I get that you should be nominated for sainthood for going through this for me—but you're still my best friend and I don't like not knowing what's going on with you." She swallowed the last bite of her wrap just as he finally took the first of his. A common theme for them.

He smirked. "What do you think I do at the ranch?"

Jillian grabbed the bag of chips from the counter, brought it back to the table, and loaded up her plate. "Exercise the horses? Clean the stalls? How the hell am I supposed to know what Wyatt has you doing?"

Monstrous, long dormant feelings surfaced with a vengeance. Even though he knew it was totally unfair to Jillian, an unexpected wave of anger and frustration swept over him. She honestly thought that he'd failed at life so hard he had to have big brother Wyatt give him a pity job? He took a deep breath. Okay, that might be a reasonable assumption after he changed his major for the third time.

But he had hoped Jillian of all people would think better of him.

"Right." He stood and emptied his half-eaten dinner into the trash, grinding his teeth as he rinsed his plate and put it in the dishwasher. "Because the baby of the family needs his family to come to the rescue, right?"

Jillian rose from her seat and laid a hand on his forearm. "Dean, I never said that. You know I think you could do anything—"

He snorted and ripped his arm away. Self-created wounds he thought had healed gaped and bled out every drop of inferiority he'd experienced growing up without the focus and determination of everyone around him.

A small voice in the back of his mind told him that this was a ridiculous reaction to a completely valid assumption on her part. But the constant, nagging inferiority complex he'd harbored since adolescence— the one that he'd thought he finally silenced when he and Mat started their venture—screamed inside his head far louder than reason.

Confused emerald green eyes stopped him and banished the pain for a brief moment. Heedless of what she'd think, what she would read into it, what he was admitting by the action, he grabbed her around the waist and pulled her flush with his body. His mouth captured hers, pouring every ounce of the confusing cascade of emotions that ran the gamut from love to frustration to anguish into the action.

He released her and a million things begged to be spoken, but he needed a clear head to do that. Instead, he grabbed his helmet and exited the front door before he said or did something he could never take back.

Dean drove around aimlessly for a few miles, then turned to point his motorcycle to the ranch. Nothing like gate crashing Wyatt and Georgia's place.

He parked his bike and pulled his phone out of his pocket. That was a jerk move and he knew it. He swiped his fingers across the screen and sent Jillian a text he hoped would help redeem him.

Dean: I'm an ass, but I'm safe at the ranch. I'll be home soon I promise.

He sent the message and put the device away before he broke down and called her. He ascended the three steps that led to the wraparound porch surrounding his brother's house and knocked twice.

Wyatt pulled open the door and his gaze swept over Dean's face. He sighed heavily. "What the hell did you do, little brother?"

Dean lifted one shoulder and sighed. "Proved that I'm a Carlisle?"

His older brother closed his eyes and groaned as he took a step to the side and held the door open wider, motioning Dean inside. "Dammit, I thought you'd be the one who wouldn't screw everything up since Jillian is used to your bullshit."

***

237

MEANT TO BE MORE

Jillian

Present Day

Ass was an understatement.

Jillian swiped the large drop from beneath her lower lid and sniffed. She curled into the corner of the couch, pulling her knees to her chest and clutching a pillow close. She made a mental note to get a cat. Or a dog. Anything furry that could handle being her emotional support.

For the first time in a very long time she was lonely. Not just alone, but lonely. Alone was something she could handle, something she sometimes craved. Alone was okay because at any second she could reach out to Dean or Angela and the dark fingers of loneliness would recede. But lonely brought back every moment of her childhood when she would sit in a room filled to capacity with people in her designer dresses and imported shoes completely ignored until one of her parents wanted to show her off to one associate or another. A vacant feeling that was her only constant companion until she met Dean.

But Angela was back in the bush with limited communication.

And Dean was...

She sighed and rested the side of her head on the back of the sofa. Dean was dealing with shit and doing it badly. Apparently he'd forgotten that she knew him better than he knew himself.

Jillian jumped up and grabbed her phone from the table where she'd left it after reading his text. Her fingers flew across the glass.

238

Jillian: Whatever lies you've been telling yourself over the past twenty years aren't true.

She tucked the device into her pocket and paced the perimeter of the living room. "Clearly he thinks I'm an idiot." She spoke out loud in the empty space, then covered her face with her hands. "Even a goldfish would be better than talking to myself at this point."

Her phone dinged to life and she grabbed it from the table.

Dean: Do you have any idea how annoying it is when you read my mind?

Her lips twitched and the tight band around her chest that barely allowed her to breathe loosened slightly.

Jillian: I'd be a really shitty best friend if I let you hide stuff from me.

She hesitated for half a second with her fingers poised over the screen, debating the merits of adding "and wife" to the message. She hit send before she fell too far down that particular rabbit hole.

Dean: I'm not mad at you, I'm mad at myself, okay? And I'm a spineless jerk for sending this by text, but I am spending the night at Wyatt's. I have early morning clients anyway and I just... I need a minute so I don't alienate my best friend completely with my own shit.

She stared at the screen and read the message three times, swallowing down the tears that threatened to spill over before giving up the fight. No one was here to witness her complete and utter decomposition.

Her heart fractured as she interpreted the silent implication. He was hurting and there was nothing she could do to fix it. Not yet.

With a deep breath, she grabbed the tissue box and loudly blew her nose. "I can't keep doing this." The whispered statement carried a heavy promise in the handful of words.

A thought wormed through to the front of her brain. She leapt off the couch, dashed into the bathroom, and splashed cold water on her face. The image reflected back at her in the mirror was most certainly not a flattering one, but certainly would do. The icy spray from the sink had worked enough magic that she didn't look like she'd been crying mere seconds earlier.

She grabbed her purse and the keys from the hooks by the door leading to the basement and the integral garage. As the initial idea grew and blossomed, the ghost of a smile played about her lips.

Twenty years of friendship replayed through her mind and tugged at her barely held together heart. Nearly hysterical laughter bubbled up at the back of her throat. "How in the hell did I ever think I wasn't in love with him?"

All of Dean's favorite things immediately popped in her head and she pieced them together with memories they had shared. Within minutes it all came together and she had a perfect vision of exactly what Dean needed to feel better.

And exactly what she needed to fortify herself to

confess the one thing she'd never told him. That somewhere along the way she'd fallen in love with her best friend and that she'd been denying it for at least a decade because losing him completely was far more terrifying than anything else.

But first...

She glanced down at the clock on the dashboard of his ridiculously small sports car. First she needed to take a stand she wasn't sure she was strong enough to make, but one that had to be in place first.

Flicking the signal on the left side of the steering wheel up, she headed down the road that led to the house she'd grown up in. Her glass castle, as Dean liked to call it. She threw the car into park in front of the massive stone stairs leading to the front door. Without any of the manners that had been drilled into her since birth, she burst inside and stalked out to the back garden where she was certain her parents were "enjoying a night cap."

Which loosely translated to getting slightly drunk together because it was one of the few things they still had in common.

"Jillian I'm shocked to see you, but—" Her mother lifted slightly from her chair, but Jillian stopped both her mother's movement and words with a sharp shake of her head.

She balled her shaking hands into fists that she concealed behind her back. "I'm sorry for barging in on you, but I needed to tell you something." Jillian took a deep, fortifying breath and said the one thing she probably should have far sooner.

"You need to contact whoever is handling your finances now and see if there is anything to save the house, your very important family legacy, because there is every chance that I won't be able to fulfill the requirements of grandfather's will." She turned to face Edward and dropped her voice to just above a whisper. "And, Father, you need to get help. Professional help."

Edward Monroe opened his mouth, but Helena got to her feet and spoke first, silencing him. "You only need to give us eighteen months. You and that boy have spent your entire childhood and adolescence doing who knows what who knows where. You would disappear from practically every function rather than behaving as the proper young lady I tried to raise you to be."

Without giving her brain time to stop her mouth, she scoffed. "You raised me? Mother, you put Frieda and Henry in charge of me the moment you could." She dug her nails into the palms of her hands and blinked against the anger-laced tears pricking the corners of her eyes. "And you sent me to every etiquette and finishing class you could find within a hundred mile radius."

Childhood memories flooded her mind, unbidden and unwanted. "You would have happily shipped me off to boarding school if Grandmother and Grandfather hadn't stopped you." Her mother's paling complexion was the fire she most definitely didn't need to urge her on. "Yes, I heard you fighting with them, telling them I would be better off thousands of miles away from everything I ever knew, everything that was familiar and comforting."

All the pain and hurt that she'd pushed down since she was little bubbled up and erupted from her mouth like a volcanic explosion. "You put on this façade that your life is devoted to charity, but only as long as it looks good, as long as you don't get your hands dirty.

But when your own *child* commits her life to going into third world countries and actually helping the people you use in pictures to drum up sympathy and donations, you act like it's a disgrace. Like *I'm* a disgrace."

She choked on a sob and turned on her heel, fleeing the monstrous building as fast as her feet could carry her. She managed to get down the driveway and a few miles down the main road before she had to pull over and let the decades of repressed emotions wash over her, streams of tears pouring from her eyes.

The only consolation she could find was the faint scent of Dean clinging to the car.

Chapter Twenty-Seven

Dean

Present Day

Footsteps coming down the stairs interrupted the speech working from Dean's brain to his mouth as he and Wyatt took their seats in the living room. An immediate broad grin broke out on his brother's face as Georgia came into view. Dean bit back a sigh.

He knew what Wyatt and Georgia had gone through to be together. He knew all too well the mistakes his brother had made leading him to very nearly not winning back the woman he loved...and left immediately after their high school graduation. But he still had a pang of jealousy mixed with longing as Georgia leaned down as far as her protruding belly would allow and gave Wyatt a kiss.

She turned to Dean and grinned. "What the hell are

you doing here? You're a newlywed, shouldn't you be home making goo-goo eyes at your wife?"

Wyatt shot his brother a knowing look and Dean dropped his head to stare at the hands clasped together, dangling between his knees for a second before he swallowed and returned his gaze to Wyatt and a silently fuming Georgia.

Her rapidly darkening glare bounced back and forth between her husband and brother-in-law until she finally let out a string of curses. She folded her arms, resting them on her swollen stomach. "You and Tanner are supposed to make sure the younger two don't screw up like you."

Wyatt held his hands up, palms out toward his wife. "Don't look at me. I told him to tell her he loves her."

With a deep groan, Dean closed his eyes and dropped his head onto the back of the couch.

"Wait, back up. What the hell are you talking about?" She shook her head before he could even respond. "Never mind, you're no help." Georgia turned her attention to Dean. "You. Tell me what the Rhinestone Cowboy is talking about."

His brother snagged Georgia's wrist and tugged her down to sit on his lap. "Although the whole avenging angel routine is hot as hell, maybe you could stop hovering over him so he can actually talk?"

Georgia's stormy expression melted slightly and she laced her fingers through Wyatt's. "You're lucky I'm a sucker for that hat."

"Okay, your over the top mushy gushy happiness is enough to turn my stomach on a normal day, but I'm currently on the verge of losing the dinner I didn't even eat, so if you could tone it down, that would be great."

Dean glared at Wyatt's responding laughter.

A plea for mama rang out loudly from the second floor of the house and Georgia groaned as she forced herself to her feet. "I'm going to get Memphis back to sleep, but I require full information later." She crossed the room and drug Dean to his feet for a firm embrace. "And no matter what you did, I'm certain Tanner and Wyatt can give you lessons on apologizing."

"Hey, who says I did anything?"

Georgia pulled back and patted his cheeks. "You're a Carlisle, and two out of three of your brothers managed to screw up their relationships. The odds are on my side." She tilted her head slightly. "But Jillian loves you, it's written all over her face. I guarantee you can make it through this."

She dropped one more kiss on her husband's lips before ascending the stairs to the rapidly growing cries from her small daughter. Wyatt's eyes tracked her every move until she disappeared up the steps.

"Seriously, Dean, what did you do?" Wyatt lifted one leg to rest his ankle on the opposite knee.

He opened his mouth, but struggled to find the words he was looking for, a way to explain it that made sense. But Wyatt had known practically since he was born that he wanted to be a bull rider and eventually open his own ranch. That was always the plan. Was there a chance in hell his brother could understand where he was coming from?

"You and Tanner and Connor..." He lifted his hands helplessly. "The three of you have always had a clear picture of your future. Hell, Jillian has too. And my dumb ass changed my major three times because I couldn't decide."

246

He got up and carded his fingers through his hair as he paced the length of the room. "Do you have any idea how it feels to be the baby who doesn't have a damn clue what I should do with my life while I sit back and watch my siblings just breathe and know what to do?"

Wyatt squinted beneath his ever present cowboy hat. "What the hell are you talking about? You and Mat have created something special, something you can be proud of. Why does it matter if it took you a few extra years to figure it out?"

"It took me years to figure out what every other person in my life just...knew. It means I'm irresponsible, unreliable, and unfocused." The statement spilled from his mouth before he could even fully formulate the thought. He dropped down onto the sofa once more. "And that isn't the kind of guy Jillian deserves. I kind of let my shit get between us tonight."

Silence followed the practically whispered proclamation and the words hung between them. It was something he hadn't admitted to himself, much less to anyone. As the seconds ticked by on the enormous clock that hung above the fireplace, he was calling himself every name he could think of for letting that particular cat out of the bag.

"Do you have any idea what it was like being next in line after the great Tanner Carlisle?"

Dean blinked rapidly, his brows furrowed together. "What?"

Wyatt let out a mirthless chuckle. "Tanner was made to take over Carlisle International. He followed in dad's footsteps to a T and managed to always make the right decisions. All-star football player, champion baseball player..." His brother shook his head. "There were

247

moments I hated his guts."

An unexpected gratitude for the understanding he never thought someone as determined as Wyatt could possibly comprehend grew in his chest. For the first time some of the weight of the burdens he'd put on himself lifted.

Dean held up his index finger. "Same. You and Connor too, just a little less."

This time Wyatt tipped his head back and gave a full, deep belly laugh. "The thing is, even though I always knew I wanted to go on the rodeo circuit, and even though I planned to open the training facility, that doesn't mean I don't know how you feel." Wyatt leaned forward at the waist, resting his forearms on his knees. "My point is that just because I've been confident in one part of my life, doesn't mean I haven't questioned things."

His older brother stood, grabbed a blanket and a pillow from the hidden closet close to his chair, and tossed them over to Dean. "The important thing is that you're doing something you love, something you're passionate about, and something you can be proud of." His lips curled into a smirk. "And I think you've seen Tanner, Connor, and even me screw up enough to know we aren't perfect. We can make a mess of our lives just as fast as anyone else."

Wyatt went to the base of the stairs and paused for a minute. "And you need to learn something I had to admit long ago."

Dean fluffed the pillow and turned to stretch out on the sofa. "What's that?"

"Gigi is always right. Jillian loves you, you just need to pull your head out of your ass long enough to tell her how you feel."

Dean spent most of the night tossing, turning, staring at the ceiling, and replaying his conversation with Wyatt. Some of the long held feelings that hung like a dark cloud over him dissipated and a bright ray of hope shone through.

Maybe he could be the man Jillian deserved.

***

Jillian

Present Day

She hadn't realized just how quickly she'd gotten used to Dean's presence beside her every night in bed until it was missing. Her heart ached with the knowledge he was hurting and her temper flared slightly at his utter stupidity in not talking to her.

Although that was a thought that damned her as much as it did him. Asking him to be the one to marry her to aid in yet another quest to be someone's saving force—although the fact it was her family, people she never expected to need her, was still a concept she found hard to grasp—was a complete no brainer. But also one of the stupidest moves of her life.

The inward groan worked its way up the back of her throat and escaped her mouth as she shoved all the supplies in Dean's car. She pressed her lips together tightly and huffed. As much as she loved the speed and responsiveness of the sports car, they'd really need to discuss having something slightly more practical than that and a motorcycle on hand.

Her heart skipped three beats. That is…if he didn't run away at even the suggestion of making their marriage a real one.

She glanced over the contents filling the front and backseats before getting inside and slowly backing out of the garage.

Whatever his answer, she would be okay. She repeated the mantra to herself over and over on the short drive, grateful for how close Dean's apartment was to his parents' home, Wyatt's ranch, and, just a little further away, Tanner's house.

A tidal wave of emotion crashed over her, unexpected tears burning the corners of her eyes. She didn't have a shadow of a doubt that she loved Dean, but it was so much more. It was his parents, his brothers…he came attached to a packaged family that filled every vacant hole left by her less than involved father and cold, distant mother. It wasn't at all surprising that he stayed nearby. They were a tight-knit clan and welcomed her into their family quickly and completely so many years ago.

She swiped beneath her lower lids. The fear of losing them as well as Dean was one of the driving factors to ignoring and denying her true feelings for him for so long.

Her stomach knotted impossibly tighter as she threw the car into park and pulled the container and bags from the backseat. Although her friendship with Dean was something she valued more than she could ever describe, telling him the truth, admitting her love, it meant that she was putting more than just that relationship on the line. She was risking losing his entire family.

She smoothed out the material in front of her and sighed. It was a chance she had to take. She laid a hand on her churning gut, surveying the scene she'd created.

A slightly hysterical, certainly stress-induced, giggle bubbled up. She had no idea how her father could have gambled so much to send their wealthy family into financial jeopardy. This one singular risk was enough to send her into an anxiety attack.

Jillian turned away with a sigh, pinning far more hope on one surprise date with her husband than she probably should. She climbed back in the car and headed to the main road, taking a left. She rolled the window down and let the warm late spring air work a little stress-relieving magic.

The archway over the drive that led to Wyatt's ranch came into view and the swarm of butterflies that had frantically been beating their wings in her abdomen multiplied and spread. A brief wave of nausea washed over her.

She parked the car near the barn and climbed out, an immediate grin spreading across her face as Wyatt came into view. "Hey there, cowpoke, any idea where I can find my husband?"

Wyatt chuckled and wrapped her in a firm hug. "He and Mat are just finishing a group session over there." He nodded to one of the farther buildings. "Then they will have a break for lunch."

Jillian drew her brows together. She wasn't certain if it were what he said or her near complete lack of sleep combined with nerves that made his words come out a jumbled mess she couldn't decipher. "Group session?"

Wyatt's lips curved up in a small, knowing smile. He held up a finger and jogged the few feet to the barn, returning with a brochure. "It may have taken him a while, but when Dean figured out what to do with his life, he went after it with everything he had and pulled Mat and myself into it." He narrowed his gaze into a mock glare. "If you tell him I said this, I'll deny it until I take my last breath, but I am so damn proud of him."

Somewhere in the distance someone called out Wyatt's name. He lifted a hand in recognition then turned back to Jillian and gave another brief embrace. "He's going to be happy to see you," he whispered in her ear before releasing her and heading in the direction of the voice.

She turned the glossy paper in her hand and then opened it. As the words registered she gasped, then put her fingers over her mouth in a vain attempt to stem the threatening tears.

Recovered Hope Equine Rehabilitation

Our unique program offers not only addiction rehabilitation and recovery services, but we integrate equine therapy with traditional counseling to give our clients a brighter hope and deeper level of empathetic care than standard rehabilitation clinics.

Two wet trails made their way down her cheeks, falling on the brochure she clutched tighter in her hand. Pride was an understatement. Her chest threatened to explode with the overwhelming flood of emotions. Dean had not only managed to find a path in life he loved, but he was changing the world around him with his work.

Voices carried across the yard from the building

where Wyatt had told her Dean and Mat were holding the group session. Despite the distance, she caught his eye and lifted one hand, curling her fingers in a small, silent greeting.

He gave one of the men a pat on the back and then jogged over to her. "Hey."

She smiled up at him, barely restraining her arms from pulling him to her and her lips from devouring his. "Can you get away for a few minutes?"

Dean flicked his wrist and looked at his watch. When his eyes dropped he caught the paper she still held firmly in her grasp. He stared at her in silence for several moments as her heart thundered behind her breastbone. "Yeah, the group will be working with the ranch hands after lunch and our final session of the day isn't until four."

Jillian laced the fingers of her free hand through his and tugged him toward the car. "Perfect, Sparky, I've got a surprise for you."

Chapter Twenty-Eight

Dean

Present Day

Dean's suspicions hitched higher when Jillian stopped them just as they reached his car, laying a hand on his chest.

"Oh, wait," she tapped a digit on his sternum, "you're missing something."

He lifted a brow. "Like all the blanks you need to fill in for me?"

She grinned up at him as she opened the car door and fished something out of the console. "When have I ever made anything that easy for you?" Jillian held up a sleeping mask between her index and middle fingers.

Dean pulled the piece of material from her. "Is this for the firing squad I definitely deserve?"

Jillian tipped her head back and laughed, soft ginger

locks falling over her shoulder. "Haven't I forced you to watch enough chick flicks for you to know that all good things start with a blindfold?"

When she reached to take the mask from him, he moved to grasp her hand in his, pulling slightly so they were only a breath apart. "I'm serious. That was an asshole move last night. I should've talked to you, should've explained. I—"

She rested the tips of her fingers on his lips, silencing his words and stealing the oxygen from his lungs. The velvety softness of every inch of her skin should have been criminal.

"Listen, Sparky, you're under some delusion I haven't been paying attention to you for the past twenty years. Like I don't know your mood swings and your behaviors better than you do." She dropped her head and a small smile curled her lips. "But I am getting way ahead of myself. Shut up and put your mask on like a good little boy." She gave him two small pats on the cheek and skipped around the front of the car, climbing in the driver's side.

Far more obedient than normal, Dean slid into the passenger's seat, pulled his door closed, and put the makeshift blindfold in place. "All right, lead me to my demise."

Silence and a quick squeeze on his thigh was the only response. Damn it. The woman had no idea she already was responsible for his complete and utter destruction. Especially if she walked away at the end.

He ground his molars together as the car jostled him around, clearly no longer on a paved road. He had to tell her he loved her. The thought had played through his mind on repeat as the dark inky sky of the night bled through into the early morning rays with him still awake and staring holes through the ceiling and out the large front window of Wyatt's house.

Dean took a deep, calming breath as the car pulled to a stop and Jillian's door opened and slammed to his left. Her soft, warm fingers curled around his hand and she pulled him out of the car and to his feet.

She stopped after a few feet, but never released her grip on him. "I missed you last night."

Her soft, whispered words landed directly in the center of his chest.

He itched to take the blindfold off, his eyes greedy to devour her, but he stood still, his thumb stroking across her knuckles. "I missed you too, Jillybean." It was the truth, but it only scratched the surface. "But I've missed you for more days than I can even attempt to count."

Finally, finally, she pulled the material free and he blinked against the noonday sun, overly bright after being in the darkness for even a few moments. The light glinted off her hair, highlighting the different shades of red and few strands of blonde and somehow managing to make her look even more stunning, a feat he once thought impossible.

Damn it all to hell, he was pretty certain he was falling farther in love with her by the day.

Just as he opened his mouth to answer, she held up a hand, palm facing him. "We need to talk." She waved her arm over to Fredrock where she'd set up a blanket covered with food and wine. "And I was trying to avoid a deep, meaningful discussion when I was both sleep deprived and hangry, so we might need to eat first."

Excitement and nerves swirled together, his gut twisting into knots, making even the thought of eating a total impossibility. Every cell in his body was pleading to hold her, but he dutifully sat down on the swatch of material instead as she piled a plate high for him and then a higher one for herself as she took the spot across from him.

Chocolate covered strawberries and small squares of brownie accompanied chocolate chip cookies and truffles. "Got a theme running here?"

"It's a comfort food. Don't judge me." She popped one of the cookies in her mouth and glared at him.

Dean took a bite of a strawberry, not even registering the taste as he chewed and swallowed. "What do you need to talk about?"

She pulled her lips inward and bit down on them. "You need to talk and I need to listen." She angled her legs and tucked them beneath her. "I want you to tell me what you do at the ranch and then I want you to tell me why it's taken this long for you to share that with your best friend."

He shook his head and looked across the water glittering in the noonday sun. One of the few times in his life he'd planned something with infinite detail and...she already knew. He'd plotted and imagined then reimagined exactly how he'd share the ins and outs of his program with her at the same time he would tell her he loved her, because the two went so perfectly hand-in-hand. But he'd seen the brochure in her hand that outlined exactly how Recovered Hope operated.

"You read all the highlights."

Jillian set down her plate and firmly clasped his free hand in both of hers. "I have waited for years for this moment. Do you honestly think I never knew how you felt? That I never noticed how every single cell in your

257

body changed anytime anyone asked what you planned to go to college for or what you were going to do with your life?"

Shock drew his gaze up to meet hers from where it had been studying the threads in the material beneath them. "I never told you."

She snorted softly. "You never had to." She drew their joined hands into her lap. "Now, tell me about your program, which I definitely haven't memorized every detail of from the brochure."

Grow a set, he silently chastised as he took a deep breath. "Actually, there *is* one really important detail that isn't in there."

Jillian wiggled her hind end so she scooted closer to him. Excitement sparkled in her emerald eyes, nearly stealing his ability to focus. "Yeah?"

He nodded. "Yeah. See, I have this best friend who is sometimes an annoying pain in the ass," he winked at her narrowed glare, "but also is the most passionate and selfless human I've ever met. She was the inspiration for me to find something bigger than myself to work toward."

Dean set his food down on the blanket to his left and cupped her cheek. He lowered his voice to being just above a whisper. "Somehow along the way to finding my purpose in life I wound up falling in love with her."

Her mouth fell open and they sat for countless moments with only the buzzing of the dragonflies and bees to break the silence.

***

258

Jillian

Present Day

"Please don't be joking." The words barely made it past her dry lips.

Dean smiled in that obnoxiously charming way she was never really able to resist and shook his head. "This isn't a joke, Jillybean. I've loved you for two decades because you're my best friend, but I finally pulled my head out of my ass long enough to realize I'm in love with you too." He lifted one shoulder. "But I needed to feel like I could be the man you deserved before I told you."

She moved to wrap her arms around his neck and plant herself firmly in his lap. "How could you ever think you didn't?"

He tucked a strand of her hair behind her ear. "I didn't have my shit together. And once I did, I had every intention of telling you everything and then..." He smirked with just a little more confidence than was necessary. "Then you came home and proposed to me."

Heat,that had absolutely nothing to do with the sun crept up the back of her neck. "Yeah, about that...I saw my parents last night. I told them that they would need to find another way to access the trust or they'd have to sell off enough assets to cover everything." She leaned her forehead against his. "I didn't want you to feel any obligation to stay married to me."

Dean tightened his hold on her waist. "This was never an obligation. I would have done anything to help you because I love you, but marrying you was a gift." He brushed his lips across hers. "One I selfishly took

259

advantage of so that I could do that whenever I wanted to."

She pulled back slightly in the circle of his arms. "Dean, I love you too, and I...I want to stay married to you for that reason and only that reason. I don't want money or misplaced familial duty to factor into it at all, so I took them out of the equation."

"You only use my real name when it's serious."

"Oh, very serious." Jillian slipped from his embrace and knelt on the dusty ground beside Fredrock. She reached around to the secret weapon she'd hidden beside the enormous stone slab. She held up the single red rose with a grin. "Will you accept this rose?"

He stood and grabbed her wrist, pulling her to her feet and fitting her firmly against his body. "I want more than a rose. I want you for real, forever." His mouth clamped onto hers, needy, passionate, demanding.

Her overloaded heart nearly exploded out of her chest at his words. She reached up to grip the back of his neck and keep his lips tight on hers.

Long moments later when they finally pulled apart, she looked up at him, the last remnants of her adolescent uncertainty still lingering in her mind. "You're sure?"

His sapphire irises melted into warm, molten pools. "For most of my life I haven't been certain of much." He dropped his head down to rest on hers. "But you have been the one thing I've never questioned."

She fisted his shirt and brought his lips back onto hers. More than a decade of the feelings she had swallowed down and tried to ignore poured into the simple action that was anything but simple. "I love

260

you." She breathed the words against his mouth. "You have no idea how long I've waited to tell you that."

Dean pulled back and tilted his head. "What do you mean?"

Jillian rolled her eyes. "You're adorable, but completely oblivious. I started falling in love with you in high school, Sparky."

His hand slipped beneath her top, stroking the bare skin of her back. His fingertips created a delicious shiver as they traveled up her spine. "What if I told you I fell in love with the seven-year-old version of you that appeared out of thin air wearing a fluffy, frothy, fancy dress?"

"I'd call you a liar." She smiled and pressed herself against him. "But that's a nice try."

His wandering digits made their way under the waistband of her pants. "You know the most annoying part of this?"

Jillian looked up at him, quirking an eyebrow. "The most annoying part of loving me?"

"Yes," he affirmed as his lips traveled from her mouth to the column of her neck. "The fact my asshole brothers were right."

Chapter Twenty-Nine

Dean

Present Day

He turned her slightly, nudging her toward Fredrock, his thumb tracing circles on her back and sending chills down his spine. He blinked once, then twice, and a third time just to be certain she wouldn't disappear in a cloud of smoke. This reality was almost too good to be true.

Jillian dropped her hand down to rest on his belt buckle. "Are we seriously doing this here? In the middle of the day?"

Dean offered her a smile filled with far more confidence than he actually felt. He couldn't admit the truth that this might be more nerve-wracking than his first time. "This is our spot, Jilly. What could be better?"

"It's also the middle of the damn day." She rolled

her eyes, but pulled his belt free of the loops with a whispered hiss. "Someone could see us."

With a gentle push of his thumb, he freed the button on her capris. "You and I both know we've spent hours out here before without anyone noticing." He gave a wicked grin as he slid the zipper down. "I guess you'll just have to be quiet so you don't draw too much attention."

She tugged his shirt free from the waistband of his pants and tossed it to her right. She pulled her bottom lip between her teeth as her fingers traced the caverns between the muscles on his chest and abdomen. "I could say the same thing to you, Sparky. You've proven to be pretty...vocal yourself."

He gently pushed on her shoulder until she took a seat on the rock and dropped to his knees to pull both of her sandals free at the same time. "That's the effect of a good woman on me." He tugged her pants down and bent to plant gentle kisses up her bare thighs.

She moaned and shed her own shirt, much to Dean's delight. His eyes feasted on his Jilly, his best friend, his lover, his wife, as she closed her eyes and tilted her head back clad only in sexy-as-hell lingerie.

"She makes me pull my shit together." He moved farther north, his lips leaving a soft trail on her skin. "She makes me fall in love." His thumb hooked beneath the band of her underwear. "And she makes me scream so loud I lose my voice."

"Oh holy hell." She laid back on the material covering the stone.

Her barely muted cries surrounded him in a melody of bliss that stretched his self-control and the limits of his jeans. Although nothing tested his resolve more than glancing up the length of her body to see her bite down on her fist as he swirled his tongue once more around the sensitive nub that he'd been lavishing his attention on.

She dug her fingers into his shoulders and pulled him up to her face. "Listen, Sparky, you better tell me you've got a condom hiding in your wallet or we are going to test the true ability of your snazzy little sports car to get us home in under five minutes."

With a soft chuckle he bent down to kiss along her shoulder to her collarbone, but his racing heart didn't miss the word "home." Their home. "My amazing wife planned a romantic rendezvous and forgot the most important part?"

Jillian palmed his cheeks, holding him just above her. "Your amazing wife was slightly preoccupied with the whole confessing her love without losing the most important person in her life thing. Sex on Fredrock hadn't really entered my mind."

He levered himself over her on one arm and reached into his back pocket, setting his wallet down beside the flaming hair fanned out around her head. "Good thing I've gotcha covered."

She shoved his shoulder until he was on his back and she straddled his waist. "Technically you're the one getting covered here, Sparky." She bent down to press a hard kiss to his lips. "And I'm just the girl to handle that."

***

Jillian

Present Day

She fished through his wallet until she located the foil pack and held it up between her index and middle fingers triumphantly. "Only one?" She rocked her hips against the denim bulge beneath her, torturing herself just as much as him. "Little disappointed in your preparedness, Sparky."

Dean groaned and gripped her waist, his thumbs moving in circles around her hipbones. "I may be a grade A specimen, Jilly, but even I require a little recovery time. At least long enough to get home."

Slowly sliding down from his body, she lifted a brow. "Listen, Sparky, we have a lot of time to make up for." She unfastened his jeans and pulled them free from his body.

His breathing shallowed as she wrapped a hand around the shaft. "We've only been married for like a week and half and sure as hell haven't exactly been celibate in that time frame. How could we have much to catch up on?"

She grinned as she planted soft kisses on his navel. "I told you, I've been in love with you for a decade. You're just a little late to the party."

Dean trembled slightly beneath her touch and her smile widened. "I stand by the statement that I've been in love with you since we were kids."

Jillian slid the latex in place slowly, with painstaking precision, and was rewarded with a guttural moan. She lifted onto her knees and hovered over him, bracing herself with one hand on his chest. With more self-control than she thought she could possess, she lowered herself onto him centimeter by centimeter, drawing out the moment as long as she possibly could.

She leaned forward and kissed his lips softly, catching the end of another tortured groan. "Doing okay there, Sparky?"

With a grunt he grabbed her waist and flipped them both until they were lying on their sides, gazes locked. "Now I am." He captured her mouth in a desperate kiss and hitched her thigh over his hip.

A light breeze floated across her bare skin, but the passion driving them both erased any chill that threatened. His steady and measured thrusts rapidly increased until he was driving inside her with the demanding force they both needed.

His fingers slid from her leg to the small of her back and pressed into her spine, keeping her flush against him. He buried his face in the crook of her neck, nipping at the sensitive skin at the juncture between her throat and neck before moving his wickedly gifted lips to her ear. "Later, I'm going to make up for this whole keeping quiet thing."

The ridiculously teasing taunt held enough seductive promise to catapult her into starry bliss. Fireworks exploded in front of her eyes and she bit her lips inward to silence the screams of ecstasy. Tremors rippled through her and she tightened her grip on his arm. Within seconds Dean's muted growls echoed through her as his body convulsed beside her.

Jillian nestled closer, her head under his chin, the rapid thumping of his heartbeat gradually returning to a steady, rhythmic cadence. She softly kissed his collarbone. "Pretty sure this whole outdoor sex thing requires further investigation."

Chapter Thirty

Dean

Present Day

As much as he wanted this moment to last forever, laying sprawled out across a rock buck naked was probably not the wisest idea. He pressed his lips to the crown of her head. "We probably need to think about moving."

She moaned and pushed into a sitting position. "I hate when you're right." She reached for her top and held it to her chest. "Any chance you'd be able to come home and get a shower before heading back to work?"

"Damn, you're insatiable." He leaned forward and kissed her shoulder before hopping off the rock to locate both of their discarded clothes. "But I think my wife's little surprise lunch necessitates getting cleaned up before going back to the ranch and pretending like absolutely nothing just happened."

Jillian hastily tugged on the undergarments he tossed her direction and searched for her shoes. "I meant so that you could be presentable for work. And good, you can help me pack up what food hasn't made its way to the ground."

Once they were both fully dressed, they worked efficiently to load everything into his car. Just as she turned to get one of the final loads he caught her in his arms and held her firmly against his body. "We're going to need to talk and figure…a lot out."

She tilted her head and looked up at him. "Like what, Sparky?"

Holding her without stupid secrets between them was like the one gift you get at Christmas that you never knew you wanted. "Like what this will mean for you. I don't want you to give up doing what you love, but I have a responsibility to manage Recovered Hope and work with Mat."

Jillian fitted herself to him slightly tighter. "I took the job Sam offered me. Working out in the field was amazing and I wouldn't trade a moment of it for anything." She cupped his face in her hands. "But right now I love what I do with Sam and I'm hoping my husband will teach me more about the program he started." Her voice dropped an octave. "And hearing you get all passionate about something is sexy as hell."

Dean groaned and pushed her slightly away from him. "You're not helping when I'm trying to have a serious conversation here." He took a step back and purposely ignored the saucy grin and lifted brow coming from the redhead. "Are you going to be good and listen?"

She rolled her eyes then tossed him a wink. "Only if I have to."

He stuck out his finger. "You have to." The last

remaining piece of the puzzle rotated in his mind. "You need to know something."

All the mischief evaporated from her face and she sobered. "Okay, I'm listening."

He took a deep breath. "I met with your dad and explained my program to him and I invited him to participate to…to try to get him some of the help he needs. I didn't think he was going to show up. I mean, he damn near kicked me out of his house, but—"

Jillian launched herself into his arms and stole his words with a soul-rending, breath-stealing kiss. He staggered slightly from the unexpected force, but held her to him, losing himself once more in everything Jillian.

"You really don't need to try to make me love you more, Sparky." She sniffed between tears rolling down her face. "I'm already crazy about you. Even though I'll still punch you if you tell anyone I was crying."

He chuckled and kept a tight grip on her. "Never, Jillybean, never. You're downright terrifying."

***

Jillian

Present Day

As soon as she turned the corner leading to their home, the sun glinted off the long black town car parked in their driveway and Jillian sucked in a breath. Dean's hand immediately appeared on top of hers from his spot in the passenger's seat.

"I'm guessing that means you didn't know they were

270

coming."

She shook her head mutely and threw the car into park along the curb. Hastily she ran trembling fingers through her hair and cast Dean a disgusted look. "I'm damn near thirty and married, and yet I am still terrified my parents are going to know I just had sex."

Dean winked, which did absolutely nothing to lessen her nerves. "Don't worry. As long as you're only having sex with your husband it's totally allowed."

A sleek head of hair the same shade as Jillian's, now liberally streaked with gray, emerged from the backseat as soon as the driver pulled the door open. Her father followed with a drawn, resigned expression on his face. "Jillian," her mother's clipped tones prickled Jillian's skin, "we've been waiting."

The instinctive urge to duck her head and apologize for making them wait washed over her, but she pushed it back and lifted her chin a notch. "Why don't you come inside, Mother?"

She blindly reached to her side for Dean and let out a small exhale of relief when his palm slid into hers and gripped firmly. Somehow she managed to unlock the door without dropping the keys in her shaking grasp.

Helena marched in behind them with Edward in tow, her gaze sweeping over their small apartment, and Jillian could practically feel the judgement radiating from her mother. "Very quaint, my dear. I'm certain this must be an upgrade compared to the tents you've been living in."

The zing of offense that shot to her spine and straightened her posture evaporated as she realized there was a...teasing note to her mother's voice. Something she hadn't really believed the woman

271

capable of.

"I like it." Jillian nodded and slid her arm around Dean's waist. "It works for us."

The older woman knitted her fingers together in front of her. Helena shot a quick look over to her husband standing at her side. "You were right."

A feather could have easily sent Jillian toppling to the carpet at the power of the three words her mother spoke. "Excuse me?"

Helena took a step toward her and some of the veneer that typically kept her perfectly expressionless face intact cracked and fell away. "I said you were right. Your father is sick. Something you would have already known if you'd allowed me to speak rather than barging in and rambling like a lunatic."

A wave of embarrassment briefly washed over her, warming her cheeks, but she lifted her chin a notch. The measure of confidence she'd gained by releasing years of pent-up hurt and frustration wiped away the momentary guilt. "I probably could have handled that better, but I don't regret anything I said."

The tight lines around her mother's eyes and mouth softened slightly before she schooled her features back into a much more controlled expression. "You most certainly could have." She nodded in Dean's direction. "Thanks to Dean, we've learned that your father's addiction is an illness and something we will need to work on for a long time."

She blinked rapidly and shook her head slightly. "But that's not the reason I'm here. It was unfair of me, of both your father and I, to lay such a heavy responsibility on you. And to ask you to do something like get married just to appease your grandfather's stipulations and access the money we needed."

Emerald eyes that mirrored her own locked on Jillian's gaze. "I can't pretend to understand your mission in life to help people you've never met, but, darling," her mother closed the few feet between them and clasped her daughter's hands tightly in hers, "I am so proud of what you've done."

Edward laid a hand on Jillian's shoulder. "*We* are proud of what you've done."

Jillian's mouth fell open and her gaze darted back and forth between her parents. "You're...what?"

"We're proud of you." The words penetrated deeper into Jillian's heart, adding small droplets to the empty lake of motherly love she'd never known before. "And your father and I managed to sit down and make massive cuts in some areas and sell off certain assets so our problems don't need to affect you anymore."

Sobs rolled through her body, unchecked and unbidden. Weight that continued to burden Jillian lifted and deep fractures inside her began to knit themselves together.

The older woman wrapped her in a warm hug, her own tears coating Jillian's shoulder. "I made many mistakes as your mother, the biggest one is that I acted like my own mother. I am so sorry, darling."

Words drifted through the fog of her consciousness, but Jillian was incapable of uttering them out loud, choosing instead to hold her mother tighter. Long seconds passed in mostly silence punctuated by sniffles and hiccups. When Helena finally released her, Jillian could have sworn they had both morphed into new beings.

"I love you, Mother." It was a phrase she hadn't

spoken since childhood, long ago learning to keep emotions to yourself.

Helena patted her cheek. "I love you too, my darling daughter." Her eyes wandered over to where Dean stood, leaning against the wall, allowing the women as much privacy as the small space allowed. "Your husband is a rather remarkable man. His guidance has changed so much for your father and I." She lifted a brow and gave him a sardonic grin. "Even if he is new money."

She pulled a cloth from the clutch she held under her arm and dabbed beneath her lids. She laid her hand in the crook of Edward's arm. "We must go now, but…Jillian, I'd love to spend more time with you."

Jillian nodded emphatically. "I'd love that too, Mother."

As her parents exited their home with a soft click of the door, Jillian launched herself at Dean again. "How in the ever loving hell did you manage all that?"

His large palm stroked up and down her spine. "Part of the program is counseling for loved ones of those who are overcoming addiction. It's a partnership, and I'm not directly involved in it, but I'd…recommended it to your mother as well. I honestly didn't believe she'd actually go."

"But she did," Jillian finished for him.

"But she did," he repeated, loosening his hold enough her feet touched the floor once more.

Jillian held his face between her palms and lifted up onto her tiptoes to plant a soft kiss on his lips. "I love you, but I'll still punch you if you tell anyone I was crying."

Epilogue

Jillian

Three Months Later

"Uncle Dean!"

Cheers went up from the pool as soon as he and Jillian stepped through his parents' sliding glass door leading to the deck. Jillian lifted her brows and he ducked his head, lifting his hands in a helpless gesture. "What can I say? Uncle Dean is a crowd favorite."

She pressed her lips together, the corners twitching with a repressed grin. "Because you are an overgrown child."

"Maybe." He gave her a quick, teasing kiss before stripping off his shirt and jumping in the water.

Jillian crossed the deck to where Georgia stood, struggling to keep newborn Savannah happy. The dark circles of motherhood rimmed the other woman's eyes and Jillian held out her arms. "Aunt Jillian is on duty now, go lay down for a bit."

The exhaustion etched on the other woman's face

melted into relief. "Wyatt and I have been taking turns at night, but then Memphis had a bad dream and only wanted Daddy and…" Her voice trailed off as she kissed her baby daughter's head. "You're a gift, Jillian."

Tracy, Izzy, and Kelsey appeared from inside, their arms laden with food. Izzy snorted at Jillian. "At least she finally listened to you. We've all tried to take Savannah at one point or another today, but she insisted we were all too busy preparing the food to have to deal with a colicky baby."

Jillian winked. "I'm just as charming to adults as I am to children." She nodded over to where Wyatt was reclining in the zero gravity lawn chair beneath an umbrella, his ever present cowboy hat tipped over his eyes, with Memphis laying across his chest, both completely passed out and oblivious to the world. "And clearly her daddy has his hands full already."

Izzy and Kelsey disappeared back inside the house with light notes of laughter following them. Tracy slipped an arm around Jillian's shoulders and looked at the younger woman with a warm smile. "I invited your parents to come over for dinner tonight."

A fresh wave of warmth and gratitude at the new relationships not only she was building with her parents, but those closest to her were as well. "She told me. Thank you so much for including them."

Tracy tsked and gave her a gentle pat. "You're family, they're family."

"Hey Jillybean," Dean called out from the pool, surrounded on every side by his nieces and nephews. "You're looking mighty fine with that baby in your arms." He gave her a broad wink and she rolled her eyes in response.

"Don't get too ahead of yourself there, Sparky." She turned, bouncing Savannah in her arms as she walked a little farther from the chaos in hopes of getting the baby to let her eyes close and stay that way.

A small smile curled her lips at the secret she would keep from him for just a few days longer until she could pull together all the things she needed to decorate Fredrock for another surprise lunch. Complete with two pink lines spray painted onto the stone slab that had always held their most precious memories.

The End

Acknowledgements

For my Double A Team, the reason I do everything, including breathe.

To my beloved hashtags and the brilliant ladies attached to them.

My #RChat lovelies, you are the reason I have a single book, much less a series. Your endless support and the lessons you've taught me have shaped my writing life. I could not have done this without you.

My #BoardmanBitches Evie & Hannah, thank you enough for living close enough to make the real life rust belt struggles bearable.

My #MDO darlings Evie, Marit, and Meka, our inappropriate jokes, half (or more than half) naked men, and adult toy discussions give me life.

To Luna for willingly being my guinea pig after major additions and sending me all the #TinyEdtor pictures and videos to brighten my day.

As always, I have to end with all the gratitude for the person—MY person—who refused to allow me to quit, told me breaks were okay, and shined a light to help me find my way out of several bouts of writer's block. Evie, I can never thank you enough for being you, for being here, and for being mine.

About the Author

Books, coffee, and chocolate make up both the heart and body mass that is better known as Amelia Foster. She has been a lifelong lover of the written word, both as a reader and an author, and completed her first manuscript at the ripe old age of five complete with illustrations. Sadly, her art was a medium that never improved over time although thankfully her writing has.

From sweet to salacious the only requirement Amelia has in books she reads–and definitely in the ones she crafts–is an excessively satisfying happily ever after…and then a little bit more.

Facebook:
https://www.facebook.com/amelia.foster.1213986

Twitter:
https://twitter.com/afosterauthor

Website:
http://ameliafosterauthor.com

Instagram:
https://www.instagram.com/ameliafosterauthor/

Pinterest:
https://www.pinterest.com/ameliafosterauthor/